Once Upon an Enchanted Kiss

An Enchanted Realms Novel

MICHELLE MILES

First edition September 17, 2024

ISBN: 9798224034734 (eBook)
ISBN: 9798989854240 (paperback)

ROTHBRIDG
STONEB
Westcliff
Myst
Kingd

odhaven
ingdom
IDGE

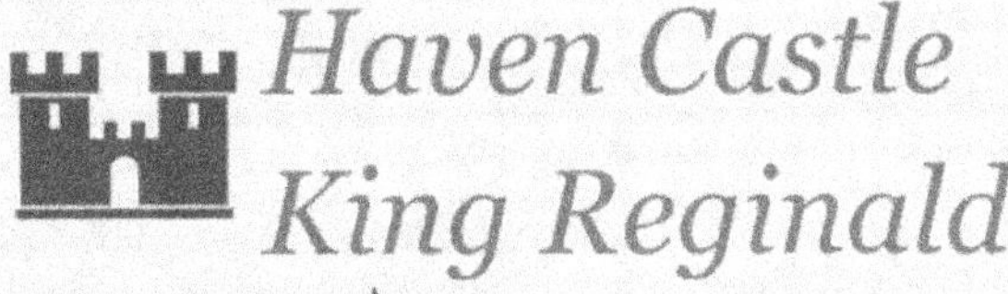
Haven Castle
King Reginald

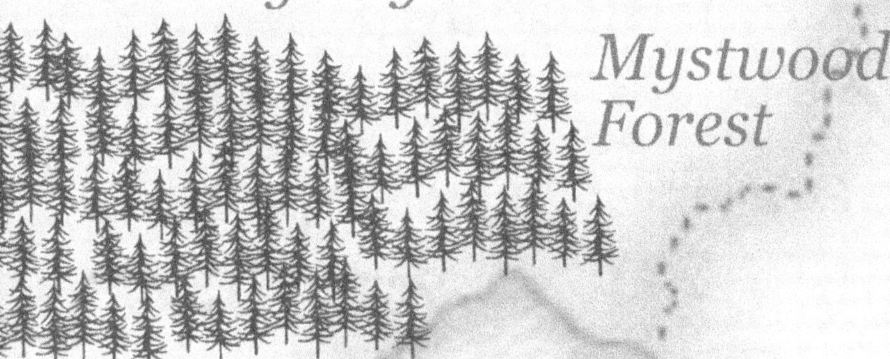
Mystwood
Forest
Briar Hill

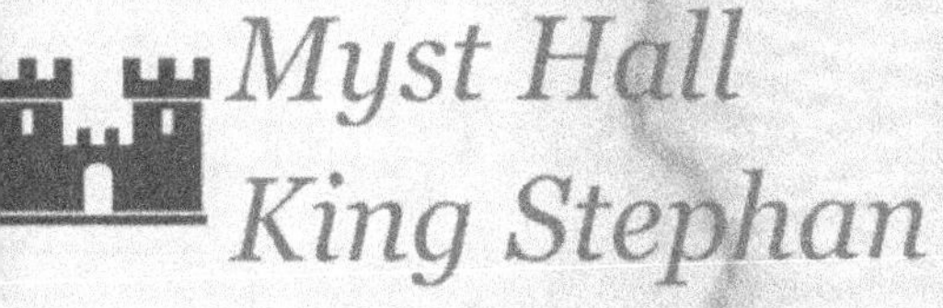
Myst Hall
King Stephan
GULF OF
CALCASTER

For my husband.

May our adventures always go wherever the wind takes us.

PROLOGUE

Late Winter, Present Day

In the darkest days of winter, when the cold was relentless and the days were dreary and cloudy, Hilde made her way to Drumchapel Village to visit her sister and niece. Snow fell in earnest as she stepped out of the cab in front of the house at 323 Crown Lane and peered up at the large white house, a sense of melancholy washing over her.

Her brother-in-law, Jack, passed away unexpectantly leaving behind his wife of thirteen years and his daughter who was nine. Now, Marigold would grow up without a father. Hilde had only spoken to her sister, Linnea, briefly on the phone when she called to give her the news. She dropped everything and returned to the village to be with her family. The only family she had left.

The sun was setting behind the house as she hurried up the walkway to the front door. She'd visited several times in the past, of course, but this time was different. Jack would not be snoozing in his favorite recliner in front of old movies.

Finally, she rang the bell. Linnea opened the door minutes later looking exhausted. Dark circles were under her eyes. Her face was devoid of makeup and her clothes were wrinkled. Almost as though she had slept in them. She gave her sister a faint smile. She reached out for a hug, holding Hilde tight before stepping back.

"I'm glad you're here." She waved her inside.

Hilde swiped the snow off her boots before entering. She slipped off her coat and hung it on the nearby coatrack as Linnea moved deeper into the silent house. Normally, the television would be on, but today it was dark and quiet.

"Would you like some coffee? I just made a pot," Linnea said.

"I'd love some."

She preferred black tea, but didn't want to make her sister do extra work. Coffee would suffice and warm her tired, cold bones. She paused in the living room, glancing around at the well-worn furniture. Jack's recliner had seen better days, the material of the chair threadbare. The floral sofa was horrible to sit on with the sinking cushions. Hilde opted for the oversized blue wing-backed chair instead.

Perching on the edge, her gaze landed on the mantle over the fireplace that was cluttered with family photographs. The three of them smiling in happier days. Before Marigold's mysterious illness forced her in and out of the hospital. Before Jack was killed in a car accident that took his life away with an abruptness that left everyone in shock. Before Linnea was left with a young daughter, a mortgage, and facing decisions about what to do next.

It pained her to think about her sister going through it all.

She couldn't allow her sister to be alone during this time.

Linnea came from the kitchen carrying two mismatched steaming mugs of coffee. She handed one to Hilde, then sat in Jack's recliner. Linnea never sat in Jack's recliner, but she understood why she did now.

"Thanks for coming on such short notice," Linnea said.

"You're my sister. I had to come. How are you?" Hilde sipped the dark brew and tried not to frown at the bitterness.

"I'm doing what I need to do." She clutched the mug between her hands, the steam rising and clouding her face.

"Are you sleeping?" she asked.

"Some." Linnea gave her a faint smile. "I'm not used to sleeping alone anymore."

"And Marigold? How is she?"

Linnea glanced upward where the girl's bedroom was above their heads. "She took it hard."

Hilde's hand tightened around the mug. "Did she have a relapse?"

"Not yet," Linnea said.

The mysterious illness came and went at will, it seemed. The doctors didn't know what was wrong with her even after running every possible test and taking multiple vials of blood. Nothing showed up on the blood work or the MRIs or CT scans.

Hilde had a suspicion what the illness could be, but she didn't dare mention it to Linnea. Her sister would deny it and refuse to believe such a thing.

Growing up, Linnea dreamed of having the perfect, picturesque suburban life. To have a house, a picket fence, kids, and a husband. Maybe a dog or a cat. And for a while, she managed to have that dream. Jack was deathly allergic to all animals, so pets were out of the question. Marigold, though, was the center of their universe. The brightest light in their life. She was their only child because Linnea was unable to bear any more children.

"Well," Hilde said at last, "I hope she doesn't."

"She's upstairs, if you want to see her. She rarely comes out of her room since the accident. I'm afraid she'll refuse to go to the funeral tomorrow," Linnea said. "I think she's in denial."

Hilde glanced at the stairs leading to the upstairs bedrooms. The last time she visited Marigold in her room was Christmas Eve when she was six and she told her the story of Ella and her Christmas prince. Perhaps it was time for another story.

Stories always made her happy.

"Maybe you can talk to her?" Linnea asked.

Hilde's gaze snapped over to her sister. "Me?"

"She loves you, you know. You're her favorite auntie." The corner of her mouth lifted in almost a smile.

"I doubt that. She has other aunts." Hilde tried another sip of coffee, then decided it was too strong for her. She placed the cup on the nearby table.

"Jack's sisters don't come to visit. Not since his parents passed." Linnea sounded almost bitter as she said it.

Jack's parents had been gone a decade. To Hilde's knowledge, he had two sisters who lived abroad.

"In fact, I'll be surprised if they show up for the funeral." Anger pinched her face as she said it.

"They haven't said?"

"No." Then she sighed. "It's just as well. We never got along. Anyway, it doesn't matter now. If they come, I'll be happy to see them. Now, about Marigold..." Her words drifted away as she gave Hilde an imploring look.

She rose from the chair. "I'll try."

"If anyone can convince her, it's you." This time, she did smile.

Hilde left the living room and headed up the stairs. She paused at the girl's door and gave a faint knock.

"I'm not hungry!" the girl shouted through the door.

Grinning, Hilde pushed open the door and poked her head through. "Neither am I."

"Aunt Hilde!"

Marigold bounced off the bed, jostling the books and papers, and ran to the door. She flung it open and fell toward her, her little arms wrapping around her in a fierce hug. Hilde hugged her back. She took her by the hand and walked back into her room.

Nine-year-old Marigold had different taste than six-year-old Marigold. Her room had changed. The princess theme was gone. The walls were repainted to a pale lavender. The canopy bed was replaced with a simple four poster twin bed. Books were scattered all over the bed. More were stacked on the floor. She had a small bookshelf in one corner that was full. Signs of a voracious reader.

"Now, let's see what you've been up to." Hilde scanned the room.

Marigold shrugged. "Just reading."

"I see." She picked up *Alice's Adventures in Wonderland*. "Ah, this is a good one."

"Have you read that?" Marigold asked.

"Indeed, I have. About Alice who follows the White Rabbit to Wonderland."

Marigold gave a wistful sigh. "I should like to go to Wonderland where there is fun and adventure."

Hilde pulled up the plush stool she'd sat on once before, still holding the book. "Why do you say that?"

"Because nothing really bad happens there." She climbed back on the bed, sitting with her back against the headboard, her legs drawn up.

"Yes, I know. But Wonderland isn't a real place." Even as she said it, she knew it was a lie.

"Well, it should be." She rested her chin on her knees, looking sad.

"Your mother tells me you don't want to go to the funeral tomorrow."

"No, I don't."

"Why not?" Hilde asked.

Instead of answering, the girl pinned her with her sad eyes and changed the subject. "Will you tell me a story, auntie?"

"A story?"

"Yes, like you always do when you visit. I want to hear a story."

She thought of the perfect story to tell her. "If you make me a promise."

Suspicion flickered through the girl's blue eyes. "A promise?"

"Yes, that you'll go with your mother to the funeral tomorrow. She's counting on you to be there with her. And so am I."

"You'll be there?" the girl asked.

"I will."

She thought about this for a long moment. "Okay. I promise."

"Good. Now. A story." She tapped her chin as though she were thinking of one to tell, even though she had already picked one out. "How about one about a prince and a princess, a sleeping curse, and a dragon?"

"Is there adventure?"

"Well, yes, of course," she said with a smile.

"Then yes!" she said.

"Once upon a time, there was a lovely princess named Rosamund..."

CHAPTER 1

O n a bright spring day in the kingdom of Myst, the queen gave birth to a perfect, healthy baby girl. King Stephan was beside himself with joy as they had long wished for a child to carry on the royal line. It was many years of waiting for them until that perfect, beautiful day.

The people of Myst rejoiced when the herald announced the happy news. A week-long festival was planned followed by a tournament. The celebration ended with an extravagant ball.

But as the days passed and the princess's christening approached, the king was restless. Stephan's most fervent wish was to see the kingdoms of Myst and Woodhaven united under one banner in the realm of Stonebridge. His great-grandfather had tried to unite the two but that had failed and ended up with them at war. Since then, each king remained within his own borders, ignoring the other.

But Stephan understood there was great advantage to uniting the two kingdoms. It would strengthen their numbers when the time came to defend themselves from Faery, their neighbor to the east whose mischievous and meddlesome Fae, he suspected, were interested in expanding their own borders.

He was aware King Reginald, ruler of Woodhaven north of Myst, had a young son. A young son who could be betrothed to his young daughter. And so, he invited the royal family to attend the princess's christening and to, he hoped, discuss the unification of the two kingdoms.

And, to show good faith, he also invited the royals from the Faery Courts—Empyrean, Celestial, Boreal, and Austral.

It was to be a grand affair.

But he made one grave error. He forgot the Fae queen from the Eternal Court.

The day of the christening arrived. All in the kingdom were invited to attend. The great hall crowded with those from the nobility and the gentry. King Reginald and his queen as well as his son, Phillip, arrived. After much debate, the two kings agreed their children would be betrothed. When Rosamund reached her eighteenth year, she and the prince would wed, uniting both the kingdoms.

Much to King Stephan's surprise, even the Fae royals made an appearance.

"You invited the Fae royals?" Reginald asked, shock evident on his face.

"I did," Stephan replied with a grin. "I had no idea they would accept much less show up."

"Impressive," Reginald said. "And perhaps you are right to unite our kingdoms. They look like a shifty lot."

There were rumblings from the Fae court for years about them wanting to expand their borders. Stephan didn't trust them one whit, but he was glad to see the arrival and hoped it would maintain peace between their realms.

Queen Titania, from the Boreal Court, arrived first in regal fashion. A stunning beauty, she was tall with perfect features that seemed to be carved by the heavens. Blonde hair shimmered under an opaque veil embossed with gold stars draping her head. The gown she wore was equally stunning and flowed around her lithe body. The dark blue material matched that of her eyes.

Next to arrive was King Draco of the Empyrean Court. As his name implied, he was stocky with thick arms and a full red beard that stopped mid-chest. He wore leather armor, as though he were ready for a war, and a gold crown with dragons carved along the edges. He sized up Titania, his beady brown eyes narrowed with suspicion.

Finally, Queen Elara of the Celestial Court and King Atlas of the Austral Court arrived within moments of each other. Each one clearly unhappy to be in the presence of the other. Elara was much like Titania, though not as regal and refined. Bright green eyes regarded the Boreal Court Queen with a look indicating she thought her counterpart was wildly overdressed for the occasion. She wore a simple gown in velvet with a gold and silver belt resting on her round hips. A matching cloak was around her shoulders. On her head, a simple silver circlet.

The four Fae rulers garnered quite the attention as they moved into the great hall heading toward the front to look upon Princess Rosamund. Stephan and his queen, Eleanor, stood at the head of the baby's rocking crib. Stephan didn't bother to hide the proud smile of a new father as they approached one by one.

Titania was first. She gazed down at the cooing baby with one slender brow raised. "Quite a…human little being, isn't she?" Then she lifted her lethal gaze to Stephan. "My most heartfelt congratulations on the birth of your princess, your majesty."

She waved her hand over the baby. A shower of glittering faery dust settled on the princess, causing her to emit a tiny sneeze.

"My gift for her is beauty and charm and grace. May she always be the most refined, perfect princess."

"Thank you, your majesty," Stephan muttered.

He and his wife exchanged a surprised glance. While he was glad the royals attended, he had never expected a gift such as that.

Then she dipped a low curtsy and moved away. Stephan watched as she took one of the seats near the front of the room, perching on the edge with her back ramrod straight.

Draco followed. He leaned over the crib and inhaled deeply which alarmed Queen Eleanor. She gripped Stephan's arm, her fingers digging into him. But before Stephan said a word, the king straightened and gave them both a broad grin.

"She's a beauty. Smells of rosewater and lilacs." His deep voice vibrated throughout the room.

Like Titania, he held his hand over the crib and sprinkled a smattering of dust. "My gift to her is one of strength and bravery. May she always face adversity with those traits."

Then he bowed deeply to them. Stephan muttered a thanks as he moved to take his seat near Titania. When she cut him a searing glance, he moved a few seats away and sat. His big body made the chair creak under his weight.

It was King Atlas who paused by the crib next. He peered down at the baby with a look of interest, one brow raised as he looked her over. Then he sprinkled a bit of faery dust over the child.

"My gift to her is intelligence and quick wit. May she never falter when she needs them most," he said. Then he looked up at the king and queen. "Felicitations to you both."

As he moved away, he eyed the seat between Titania and Draco. Though she gave him a withering look, he ignored it and placed himself between them without so much as a sideways glance.

Finally, Queen Elara moved to stand next to the baby. She placed her hands on the crib and gave it a gentle nudge, watching as it rocked slowly. Princess Rosamund gurgled her approval of the movement, waving tiny fists in the air.

"She's lovely," Elara breathed. "Indeed, she will be beautiful and strong and intelligent. For my gift—"

The doors to the great hall banged open, interrupting her. All turned to see a figure with the sun at her back standing in the doorway. She was nothing but a silhouetted outline as she stood there. Whispered questions hissed through the great hall.

It was Queen Elara who inhaled a sharp breath and whispered, "Rowena." She snapped her head in the direction of King Stephan. "Did you invite the Queen of the Eternal Court?"

A sickly sensation pierced Stephan as he looked at the figure standing in the doorway. His mouth went bone dry.

"I...I think she was overlooked."

"Oh, dear," Titiania said as she rose to her full height. "A grave error, indeed."

Atlas and Draco also got to their feet, turning to eye the queen at the end of the great hall.

Rowena sauntered from the doorway in slow, methodical, purposeful steps. Dark, baleful eyes alighted on the crowd as she went. She was dressed in a long-sleeved gown of shimmering midnight, a long train trailing behind her. Circling her head was an onyx crown that glittered like mirrored shafts of light. Angled cheekbones and full dark red lips gave her face a severe appearance. There was something sinister, yet beautiful about her. At the end of the aisle, she paused, her sharp gaze glancing from King Stephan and his wife to the baby nestled inside the cradle.

Silence descended on the gathering.

"Well, isn't this a lovely affair."

Her voice echoed throughout the great hall. Glittering black eyes paused on each of the Fae royals before resting on King Stephan.

"Pity I didn't garner an invitation. Though I was able to find my way here after all."

"Your majesty, my deepest apologies," King Stephan said as he stepped around Queen Elara. He grappled with an excuse—any excuse—that would appease the dark queen. "Your kingdom is remote and—"

"Remote?" She laughed but it was without humor. "Perhaps you feel that way because it's on the other side of the kingdom from..." she paused, gave a look of disdain and waved her hand at the other royals, "...them."

"We want no trouble here, Rowena," Draco said, stepping forward. He paused next to Stephan.

She flashed him a look so deadly, he pressed his lips together into a straight line. Queen Eleanor stepped forward then, placing herself between Rowena and the baby. Stephan reached for her but she waved him off.

"We meant no disrespect, your majesty," she said, her voice even and clear. "We would be pleased if you joined us."

"Would you?" One dark brow lifted in question.

"Of course." Eleanor gave her a smile. Then she did the unthinkable. She held her hand out to the dark queen. "Come and meet our new princess."

Rowena's gaze landed on the crib. She walked forward, ignoring Eleanor's outstretched hand. The queen dropped her hand as Rowena peered down at the tiny baby with the waving fists in the cradle. The little princess's skin shimmered with faery dust from the other three royals bestowing their gift upon her.

"What a lovely child," she said. "I see the others have imparted faery gifts. Allow me to bestow *my* gift upon the princess."

Eleanor, still smiling, said, "We would love that."

Rowena bent over the crib and drew her finger down the baby's cheek. Her skin still glittered with faery dust.

"Little princess, I see you have been given gifts of beauty, strength, and charm." She straightened, then held one of her hands down, cupped. A swirling shimmery cloud of purple magic was contained in her palm as she lifted it up. Her gaze met the king's. "But none of those will be enough to save her, for before the sun sets on her eighteenth birthday she will prick her finger on the thorn of a rose...and die."

As she spoke the last two words, she blew the shimmery purple faery dust. It trickled down and landed on the baby, who immediately cried out. Eleanor gasped as she reached for the baby, but it was too late. Atlas and Draco both pulled their weapons, their swords pointed at the Queen of the Eternal Court. Even Titania looked distraught at the curse that was placed upon the young princess.

"Arrest her!" Stephan ordered his guards.

But as they charged forward, Queen Rowena disappeared in puff of purple haze. Eleanor, tears in her eyes, held the wailing baby.

King Stephan turned to the assembled Fae royals. "The curse. Can it be reversed?"

Titania shook her head. "I'm afraid not. Rowena's dark magic is powerful. But fear not, King Stephan, Queen Elara has yet to give her gift to the baby."

Queen Elara shot Titania a surprised glance before understanding dawned. Nodding, she moved to stand next to Eleanor, placing her hand on the crown of the baby's head. Her crying stopped.

"Dear princess," Elara said, her voice soft and soothing. "Indeed, you will grow into a beauty with charm and grace. You will be strong and brave. Should you prick your finger on the thorn of a rose before the sun sets on your eighteenth birthday you will *not* die. Nay, you will fall into a deep slumber."

Elara leaned down and whispered something, then placed a kiss on the baby's forehead. A shimmering white light surrounded both of them. When she stood straight, she granted Queen Eleanor a reassuring smile.

With that, the four Fae royals bid King Stephan and his court farewell.

In an effort to keep his daughter safe, King Stephan ordered the removal and destruction of every rosebush in and around the castle. He hoped it would be enough.

CHAPTER 2

Eighteen years later

Princess Rosamund sat in the sewing circle, holding the embroidery hoop while staring out the window. It was a perfect spring day with a bright blue sky and a few wispy clouds. The twitter of birdsong filtered in through the open casement and somewhere below in the castle gardens, a squirrel emitted an angry chatter. It was followed immediately by the caw of a mockingbird that wanted nothing to do with the squirrel.

Or so she imagined.

It was a picture-perfect day for riding or running through the gardens barefoot with the wind in her hair.

"Rosamund, your sewing," her mother chastised.

Her mother nudged her with her elbow. With a sigh, she went back to the linen pulled taut in the hoop and stabbed it with the needle, tugging through pale pink thread and pretending she was interested in embroidery. She wasn't.

All she wanted to do was run through the iron gate in the castle gardens and into the meadow just beyond the walls to freedom. To smell the fragrant blooming flowers and lay under the willow tree in the cool grass. To dance pebbles over the stream and watch them skip.

Instead, she was stuck inside within the sewing circle with her mother, the queen, and her ladies in waiting and all the other courtly women who were busy gossiping about anything and everything. The servants, their husbands, their children, whoever. When they tired of gossip, they turned their conversation to the latest fashions coming out of Rothbridge, the realm to the north. Apparently, there were luxurious silks and velvets that all the ladies were mad to have.

The dressmakers, it seemed, had trouble keeping up with demand.

Rosamund was bored out of her head. She cared not for silks or velvets or the latest fashion in hats.

Though she was a princess, she wasn't interested in sewing or singing or dancing or anything else that taught her to be the perfect, proper princess. Her parents kept a close eye on her, never letting her out of their sight. And if they weren't available, then any one of the servants or guards would be her constant companion.

It was exhausting.

Her interest was in riding her favorite horse, a beautiful gray mare. She longed for adventure and excitement and fun. Not sitting inside a drafty castle forever.

As her eighteenth birthday approached, all she needed now was a line of suitors to come knocking on the door to ask for her hand in marriage. She was certain her father was busy trying to make the perfect match for her with one of the nobles. A duke would be his first choice. He'd settle for a marquess or an earl. He'd absolutely refuse a viscount or a baron. She was a princess, after all.

As she stabbed the material once again, the faint sound of a trumpet wafted through the open window on the breeze. Her head snapped up. She glanced at her mother, who seemed not to notice as she continued with her perfect stitches.

The trumpet sounded again. Rosamund dropped her sewing and hurried to the window.

"Did you hear that?"

She stood on tiptoe and leaned out. But there was nothing to see but the castle gardens.

"Ah, yes," her mother said. She stood with a rustle of skirts. "Our visitors have arrived. Come, Rosamund. We must greet them."

Rosamund whirled from the window and gaped at her mother. "Who is it?"

Her mother handed off her sewing to one of the ladies and waved for Rosamund to follow her. She didn't bother to answer her question.

Curious, she followed her out of the room, glad to have the sewing circle behind her. If there were trumpets, then the visitor was of some importance.

They made their way down the curved staircase and to the great hall, where the servants were lined up in perfect order from the door which was open to welcome the visitor. Her father was outside, standing at attention dressed in his finery.

Rosamund glanced down at her simple gown of blue muslin, then over to her mother. She wore a pale lavender gown trimmed in lace and held her hands clasped in front of her, standing rigid and tall.

Her mother's blonde hair was coiled about her head with ringlets on each side of her comely face. She had a regal look about her with high cheekbones and full lips under a thin, straight nose.

Rosamund straightened and did her best to mimic her mother, but she was not nearly as regal or refined. Her hair hung in waves down her back. Her cheekbones were not nearly as high and her lips were certainly not perfect. The only thing she got from her mother that was perfect was her dark green eyes.

The carriage rumbled up the dusty path heading for the castle. It was not ornate or ostentatious. Just a simple carriage drawn by four trotting horses. Rosamund glanced at her mother who stood still, her keen eyes on the carriage in the distance. Her stoic face was devoid of emotion.

The carriage came to a halt. The footman stepped down to open the door and stand aside. A man emerged. He turned back to the carriage, his hand outstretched to help the woman step down. Her father remained in place as the couple approached. Something about them told Rosamund they were not merely from the nobility. They were more. They were royalty.

But the only royals she knew of were the ones to the north in the kingdom of Woodhaven. As far as she knew, they simply weren't that friendly with each other. But perhaps something changed.

"Ah, Reginald. It's good to see you again." Her father stepped forward, extending his hand.

Reginald took it, gave it a shake. "And you, Stephan. You remember my wife, Adele?"

"Yes, of course. It's a pleasure to see you again." He took her hand and kissed it, then turned and motioned to her and her mother. "And you remember my wife, Eleanor, and my daughter, Rosamund."

Her mother stepped forward, a warm smile on her face. Rosamund followed her lead as questions floated through her mind. Why would the king and queen of Woodhaven come here? Why would her father invite them?

"Nice to see you both again, your majesties," her mother said, dipping a low curtsy.

Reginald gave a hearty laugh that rumbled deep in his throat and jiggled his ample belly. "No need to stand on ceremony with us." When he spotted her, he grinned so big, his eyes lit up. "Ah, princess. I haven't seen you since you were a babe. You've grown into a fine young woman, haven't you?"

She said nothing as she peered at the man she didn't know. He was short and stocky with a thick middle and a full white beard. His hair was neatly combed under the simple gold crown. He wore a dark blue tunic, black breeches, boots covered in dust, and a cloak around his shoulders clasped with a gold pin.

"Of course, she has," the queen of Woodhaven said as she shoved aside her husband. She reached for Rosamund's hand, holding it in her soft one. A small smile creased her lips. "We're glad to see you, my dear."

Rosamund didn't understand what all the fuss was about. She merely granted the woman a smile and dipped a quick curtsy.

The queen was tall and regal and beautiful. Far too beautiful for the stodgy king. Her dark hair was pulled back in one long braid hanging down her back. She wore a matching gold crown on her head and dangling earrings that seemed to accentuate her long neck. Her gown was a deep purple muslin with lace at the elbows and she exuded a calm confidence, much like her mother.

Perhaps that was the requirement to be queen.

"It's nice to make your acquaintance, your majesty," Rosamund said, finding her voice at last.

Adele chuckled, then said to her mother, "She's a darling girl."

"But where is Phillip?" her father asked, peering into the empty carriage.

Reginald cleared his throat loudly. "Couldn't make it this trip."

"What my husband isn't telling you is he's off on some hunting expedition." Adele gave a pinched expression, clearly unhappy with that idea. "He'll be along in a few days."

"Pardon me," Rosamund said, "but who is Phillip?"

"Why, my dear, he's our son, the prince," Adele said with a grin. "Your betrothed."

CHAPTER 3

Rosamund stared in shocked silence at the queen. "My what?"

Her mother wrapped an arm around her shoulders and steered her away from Queen Adele back into the castle. But Rosamund was having none of that. She shrugged out of her mother's embrace and spun to face her. Her heart thudded against her chest.

Certainly, she understood what the word *betrothed* meant. However, she never expected her future husband was the prince of their neighboring kingdom. A kingdom, she understood, that was their enemy.

No, enemy was too strong a word. Perhaps they were more of a rival kingdom.

"What does she mean my betrothed?"

"Just that," Reginald said, following them inside. "You're to marry my son, Prince Phillip."

The heat of shock coiled through her, making her gut clench. She glanced from the rotund king back to her mother. "You never told me this."

Adele didn't bother to hide her gasp of surprise.

Her tone was accusatory. Her mother gave a half smile and reached for her again, but Rosamund stepped away.

"You never told her?" the queen asked. "Why ever not?"

Rosamund crossed her arms over her chest. "Yes. Why not, Mother?"

"Eleanor, please," her father said, his tone hushed and urgent. It was a desperate plea to get her away from the visiting royals, no doubt.

"Come, Rosamund and we will discuss it." Her mother held her hand out to her.

She stole a quick look at the other royals, then her father, who had a desperate look on his face. At last, she reached for her mother's hand and took it. She grasped it, wrapping her fingers in her tight fist and pulling her along behind her. It was clear to Rosamund her mother wasn't going to release her.

She led Rosamund from the great hall through the castle, up the winding stone staircase, to her private sitting room. The queen enjoyed this room daily with its balcony and the gossamer curtains billowing at the windows and open doors. She often had tea here in the afternoon with tiny sandwiches and lemon cakes.

The room was furnished in plush, comfortable chairs, a chaise, a luxurious rug in a floral pattern that came from Rothbridge in vibrant colors of red, yellow, green and blue. A fireplace was on one wall to warm the room in the chillier months. When they were safely inside the room, her mother closed the door and motioned for her to sit. Then she went to the gold cord and rang for tea.

Rosamund waited, watching with her breath in her throat as her mother pulled open the balcony doors. The fresh spring breeze trickled in, giving the stuffy room a breath of fresh air. She stood there a long moment, her back to Rosamund. She was stiff, the muscles pulled taught under her gown.

The princess perched on one of the chairs, her hands in her lap, her ankles crossed like a proper lady, and waited.

Finally, her mother turned to her, her face flushed. "I see it was a mistake not to tell you sooner. For that, I ask your forgiveness."

Rosamund stared at her mother, who, for the first time in her life, seemed to be at a loss.

"However," she continued, and her voice turned stern, "you are never to act like that in front of the king and queen of Woodhaven again."

Before she could stop the words, she said, "Act like *what*, Mother? Like I was in shock? Because I was."

She clenched her jaw so tight, the muscles flexed along the edge. Her lips thinned. Clearly, she was trying to contain her anger.

"You are never to question me or your father in front of the other royals," she said, her voice hard.

"Then perhaps, Mother, you tell me exactly what's going on." She folded her arms over her chest. "I deserve to know."

Her mother blew out a breath and turned back to the balcony, the slight breeze ruffling her hair and skirt.

"You do deserve to know," she said, her voice quiet. "Your father didn't want to tell you until you were of age."

"Of age?" she asked.

"You turn eighteen soon."

"Yes, I'm aware." Irritation clawed through her as she peered at her mother's perfect posture.

Before her mother answered, a knock sounded on the door. She called for them to come in. The servant wheeled in the tea cart with a silver tea service and porcelain cups rattling as he pushed it across the floor. Rosamund spied the tiny finger sandwiches and lemon cakes next to the tea and her stomach rumbled. She'd forgotten to eat breakfast.

"Thank you, Albert," her mother said in her dismissive tone.

He gave a brief bow and scurried out of the room, closing the door behind him.

Her mother moved to the cart and poured a cup of tea. She placed two lumps of sugar in the cup and stirred. She didn't offer Rosamund a cup.

She waited to see what her mother would say next.

"When you were six months old, your father invited the royals of Woodhaven to treat with us," she said. She held the cup between her hands, then blew on the steaming liquid.

Rosamund waited, peering at her with interest. She seemed genuinely unnerved.

"Your father believes the Fae royals have an interest in expanding their borders," she continued. She cut her daughter a sharp glance. "I trust you are familiar with the geography of the land."

Rosamund stifled the snort. Instead, she said, "Of course, I am. They're the realm to the east."

"Yes," her mother said, then took a sip of the steaming tea. "In an effort to unite the kingdoms of Stonebridge, your father offered your hand in marriage to Prince Phillip of Woodhaven. King Reginald agreed. You are to be married shortly after your eighteenth birthday."

Had they been planning her wedding all this time without telling her? Rosamund stared at her mother in shocked silence.

"My birthday is in a week," she said.

"It is," she said, her face devoid of all emotion. "All the wedding arrangements have been made. All we have left to do is fit you for your gown."

Panic began to set in, her heart pounding so hard in her chest she thought it might burst. There were so many things wrong with this situation, she didn't know where to begin.

"I suppose that's already been decided for me as well." A bitter taste was in the back of her throat.

"It has."

"I don't want to marry a prince I've never met." It was the first thing that came to mind.

"You were supposed to meet today. That is why they came. And yet..." Her words trailed off.

"He decided hunting was more important." Rosamund almost laughed out loud.

How fortunate for him that, as a man, he could run free and do as he pleased. While she was forced into a marriage in which she had no interest. Forced to participate in a wedding she had no input in planning. Forced into a life she didn't want.

"They also came to finalize the plans for the wedding," her mother added.

She shot to her feet. "And I'm just supposed to be okay with all of this?" Rosamund demanded.

Her mother plunked the tea cup down on the tray with a thud, the ire in her face evident. "You are a princess, Rosamund. It is what was agreed to between your father and King Reginald. You are to marry Prince Phillip."

She clenched her fists so hard, her nails bit into the palms of her hands. "And I have no say in this whatsoever?"

Her mother straightened, looking down her nose at her and giving Rosamund her most regal look. "You do not."

Rosamund inhaled a breath, then blew it out slowly. "Very well, Mother. If that's what you and Papa wish, then so be it. I will marry the prince. But know this. I will never love him. I do this out of duty to my kingdom and nothing more."

"That is the price of being a princess," her mother said.

Her words cut deep. Rosamund spun on the toe of her slipper and stomped to the door.

"Where are you going?" her mother asked.

She paused at the door, her hand on the knob, and cut her mother a glance over her shoulder. "Nowhere, Mother. I have nowhere to go."

She flung open the door and left.

CHAPTER 4

Fury beat through Rosamund as she charged down the stairs and through the great hall, her mind on one destination only. Her father and the Woodhaven royals were in the great hall, discussing the upcoming wedding. When Queen Adele tried to engage her, she breezed past her, ignoring her.

"Rosamund!" her father called.

But she ignored him too, still gripping her skirts tight in her fists and nearly sprinting through the halls.

"Forgive her, your majesty," she overheard her father say.

"No need. She's had a bit of a shock, I gather," the queen responded.

Her father said something else, but Rosamund was out the door and into the hall and didn't hear. Her eyes were blurred with tears as she picked up speed. She charged into the royal gardens, never stopping until she was a good distance from the castle. She paused to swipe at the tears in her eyes.

The gardens were fragrant this time of year, since it was spring. There were lilacs, chrysanthemums, tulips, and lilies in bloom. As she stood on the path, she surveyed the immaculate grounds and wondered, not for the first time, why there were no roses.

From what she gathered from the groundskeeper roses were forbidden to be grown in the royal gardens. Or anywhere near the castle, for that matter. She never understood why. She had never seen one or smelled one. She only knew about roses from pictures in books and reading about their sweet, perfect fragrance.

With slow steps, she headed to the gazebo where she liked to spend time alone to think. She sat on the bench, staring out at the swaying bushes of flowers.

She didn't want to marry someone she had never met. Certainly, she understood she was to be betrothed at some point but she did not expect to have already been betrothed her entire life. All this time, she thought her father was planning which nobles to bring to the castle to meet her and ask for her hand when instead he was secretly planning her wedding and her future.

A future with a prince from that *other* kingdom. What was she to do? It was impossible to refuse and shirk her duty as princess. Her parents would never allow her to deny the hand of a prince.

Some part of her, though, had hoped she would marry for love instead of duty. That hope was utterly squashed.

Though Queen Adele and King Reginald seemed to be cordial, intelligent people, she was still not interested in marrying their son. Even if he was just as cordial and intelligent.

As she brooded, something fluttered near her face. She realized it was a dragonfly with iridescent wings that beat so quickly, they were a blur. The dragonfly alighted on the nearby railing, the wings slowing to nothing more than a faint flutter.

"Why so melancholy, princess?" a high-pitched voice nearby asked.

She startled, glancing around to see who was speaking, but there was no one there. She was alone. She stiffened, her back ramrod straight.

"Who's there?" she demanded.

The dragonfly remained where it was. "It's me."

She glanced around again, this time scooting to the edge of the seat. But still there was no one there.

"Down here," the voice said.

She peered at the small winged creature as its wings moved up and down in slow methodical beats.

"Hello," it said, a smile in its voice.

How could a dragonfly *smile*?

"You?" Rosamund moved closer to inspect the creature.

It chuckled. "Yes, of course."

"You can talk?"

Another chuckle. "All creatures can. You just have to know how to listen."

Rosamund shook her head as she perched on the bench near the dragonfly looking at it in wonder. "Amazing," she breathed.

"So, tell me, princess, why are you sad?"

She leaned back in the seat, her back pressing into the wood gazebo, and sighed. "I'm to be married."

A small flutter of wings, then, "Is that so terrible?"

"It is when you've never met the other person," she said, sounding glum.

"Ah, I see. And you do not wish to marry this person?" the dragonfly asked.

"Prince," Rosamund said. "He's a prince of the neighboring kingdom. And, no, I do not." Again, she let out a heavy breath. "I suppose there's nothing to be done about it, though."

"Why not?"

"Because I am a princess, and I must obey my parents' wishes."

"Must you?"

Rosamund looked down at the creature. "You are a dragonfly. You don't understand."

It rose up and fluttered close to her face. "You could always leave."

The princess tipped her head to one side. "Leave?"

"Yes. Pack a bag, leave the castle, never look back."

Her heart picked up speed. "You mean, run away?"

"I mean find a life of your own," the little dragonfly corrected. "The world is a big place, after all."

Rosamund considered this. She stared down the path toward the castle, wondering if that was something she would be able to do. Pack a bag and leave. Never look back. Forge her own way. Live her own life. But how? She knew nothing of the world outside the castle walls. She had barely spent time outside them her entire life. Her father kept her closely guarded. He refused to let her ride alone. She always had an escort.

"Perhaps it is a bad idea," the dragonfly said and alighted once more on the railing.

Rosamund's pulse quickened as she thought of leaving.

"It's a wonderful idea," the princess whispered.

She pressed cold fingertips to her lips, imagining what it would be like to leave this place behind. To become her own person. To marry for love instead of duty. Or perhaps not marry at all. The more she thought about it, the more her heart pounded with excitement.

She shot to her feet suddenly, then turned to the dragonfly still on the railing. "Thank you."

"For what?"

"For the advice." Rosamund flashed her a smile and then took off running back up the path toward the castle, her skirts in her fists.

She was going to pack a bag, wait for the cover of nightfall, and then leave this place forever.

When the princess was at the end of the path, the dragonfly rose up from the railing and, using a bit of magic, turned back into her true form. Queen Rowena watched her go, a deep guttural laugh bubbling up her throat.

"You are so welcome, princess."

Her plan worked beautifully. Now all she had to do was give the girl a little push and she'd prick her finger on a thorn in no time.

Grinning, she waved her arms and disappeared in a puff of magic, returning to her home deep in the Eternal Court.

CHAPTER 5

Prince Phillip grabbed the tankard of ale and quaffed it, the liquid trickling down his chin as he did so. Then he thumped it back down on the table, grinning at his best mates. They cheered his ability to drink the pint in one gulp.

"Your turn, my friend," Phillip said to Jeffrey, his best friend.

Jeffrey scowled as he grabbed the tankard in one hand. Charles and Phillip both cheered him on, but Phillip had the broadest grin of all. Around them, the tavern was a buzz of activity. None of the other patrons paid them any mind and the bartender didn't realize the Crown Prince of Woodhaven was sitting under his roof.

Lord Jeffrey lifted the tankard and started to drink. Halfway through, he choked and slammed it down on the table with a loud thud. He huffed out a breath, his head falling to the table as he gulped in breaths. Phillip and Charles laughed.

"Maybe next time, old friend!" Phillip said, patting him on the back.

Jeffrey lifted his head and wiped his chin with the back of his hand, glaring at him. "Show off," he muttered.

"Indeed, I am," he said, sounding jovial.

"I'll get us another round," Charles said, rising and heading over to the bartender.

Phillip didn't have the heart to tell him no. He was having too much of a good time. He leaned back in his chair, balancing it on the back two legs and watching the crowd around them. The tavern was packed this time of night with all types of men—and some women, too. Fisherman and hunters mostly. He and his friends spent the afternoon pretending to hunt pheasant. In truth, they killed nothing. He was windblown and tired, but happy.

Jeffrey ran a finger around the rim of his half-full tankard watching him watch the tavern.

"So, when are you going to fess up?" he asked, cutting him a glance.

"Fess up?" Phillip replied, his brows furrowed in question as he looked at him.

He and Jeffrey were friends their entire lives. They grew up together from the crib to now. They played cards together, gambled, chased women, hunted, fished, and everything in between. He dragged along his younger brother, Charles, on most of the hunting excursions.

Jeffrey leaned close and said, "The betrothal."

Instantly, Phillip's mood darkened. He frowned down into his empty tankard, wishing Charles would hurry with the next round.

"I don't want to talk about it," he said.

"Because it's nearly time, isn't it?" Jeffrey teased. "You and I both know the time of the wedding approaches. Aren't you supposed to be in Myst Hall right now?"

"I *said* I don't want to talk about it."

Charles returned with three tankards and plopped them down in the middle of the table, the froth swishing over the edges.

"Talk about what?" he asked.

Before Phillip could answer, Jeffrey said, "His wedding."

Charles's face lit up in a bright smile. "You're getting married?"

"Shh," Phillip said, sitting forward. The front legs of the chair banged against the floor. "Keep your voice down."

"Isn't this a time for celebration?" Charles asked, still completely oblivious to Phillip's annoyance.

"No, it isn't," he groused.

"It is," Jeffrey corrected. "He just doesn't want to admit it."

"Why not?" Charles lowered to the chair opposite Phillip and slid one of the tankards toward him.

"Because it's an arranged marriage," Phillip said. "I've never even met the girl."

"That's not true," Jeffrey corrected. "You *have* met her."

"Meeting her when she was six months old does not count," he snapped.

He remembered the day well. He and his parents had traveled to the Myst Kingdom to witness the christening of the princess. At the time, Phillip was six years old and was more interested in riding his horse and shooting his bow and arrows than anything else, much less attending a boring thing like a christening. In fact, he was bored most of the trip and even more bored when he was forced to stand at attention next to his parents during the ceremony. When he fidgeted, his mother pinched his earlobe to make him stop.

He recalled with some clarity the Fae royals arriving in grand fashion. It was somewhat of a special occasion as the Fae royals never left their own Courts for anything. But somehow, King Stephan had enticed them to come to the baby's christening. His father said it was an invitation of good faith because, for whatever reason, King Stephan believed the Fae wanted to invade Stonebridge and expand their borders.

His father, however, thought that was nothing but folly. Even so, he had agreed to marry Phillip off to the princess. A cherub faced little squirming thing with pink skin.

Honestly, he never thought his father would go through with the betrothal. The last few weeks, though, he and his mother pestered him about the wedding and visiting Myst to meet his bride now that she had almost come of age. She would be eighteen soon and then they would marry.

It was why he snuck out early one morning with Charles and Jeffrey to go on a hunting expedition. A hunting expedition that was really nothing more than him avoiding his royal duties.

"So, when do you meet her for real?" Charles asked.

He had no idea what was going on inside Phillip's head as he brooded about the betrothal.

"He's supposed to be meeting her now," Jeffrey said in his most helpful voice.

"He is? But he's hunting with us."

"And that's exactly *why* I'm hunting with you." Phillip reached for one of the tankards in the center and pulled it to him, frowning down into the amber liquid.

"You have to face it at some point," Jeffrey said, a broad smile on his face.

"No, I don't."

Jeffrey chuckled. "Your mother asked me to escort you to Myst."

His head snapped up. He gaped at his friend. "When did she ask you that?"

"Before we left, actually." He took a sip of his ale. "She said I should let you have this one last..." he paused, searching for the word, "adventure, but then to please make sure you arrive at Myst Hall in a timely manner."

Phillip scowled. He clutched the handle of the tankard and then quaffed the entire thing in one long gulp.

"It's amazing that you can do that," Charles said, his voice tinged with awe.

Phillip slammed down the tankard, then looked at his friend. "It's a gift." He took in a deep breath, then blew it out. "Perhaps it's time for me to return home and prepare for my…" His words drifted off.

"For your upcoming nuptials?" Jeffrey chuckled. "I heartily agree."

"Oh, can I come too? I'd love to see Phillip wed at long last," Charles chided.

"*You* can stay home," Phillip growled.

Charles merely laughed. "If you insist, your highness. Won't all the ladies of the court be devastated when they learn you're spoken for?"

Jeffrey laughed at that. "They indeed will! Perhaps I'll take your place as the resident rogue."

Phillip glared at his friend, then gave him a devilish grin. "You can try, my friend. You can certainly try."

But Phillip had no intention of going to Myst Hall. In fact, when they returned home, he would find a way to slip into the night, away from the castle. He wasn't interested in court politics or a betrothal to a princess he'd never met. What if she'd grown up to be a troll? No, he would find his own way.

He'd pack a bag and leave behind the castle and his princely title forever.

Chapter 6

Rosamund was required to attend dinner with her parents and the visiting royals that evening. She was a ball of nervous energy as she sat at the table through each and every course, her hands clasped in her lap when she wasn't eating. Her mother eyed her from across the table, clearly aware of her fidgeting.

She gave her one of her motherly looks that indicated she wanted her to stop.

Rosamund stilled her hands in her lap and put on her best calm face. But her mother likely suspected she was up to something. And she was.

That afternoon, when she returned to her room, she paced the length of it, trying to decide what to pack. Certainly not gowns. They wouldn't do if she were to go into the woods or even one of the local villages. She didn't need to look like a princess. She needed to look like a commoner.

When her maid, Lucy, arrived to dress her for dinner, she eyed the girl up and down and realized with some hope they were close to the same size. Rosamund was a bit taller than she was but even so, she was sure her plan would work.

Well, almost sure.

After dinner, she planned to make her way into the kitchen to filch whatever food she could find to take with her. Since she didn't know where her next meal would come from, she wanted to be prepared. She also thought about grabbing a water skin to take with her. Then her plan was to sneak into Lucy's room and take one of her rough-spun gowns to wear.

"Rosamund?" Her mother's voice snapped her out of her thoughts and she startled.

"Yes?" She sat up straighter and looked at her mother across the table.

"Queen Adele asked you a question." Her mother's eyes glinted with annoyance.

"I'm sorry. I didn't hear it. What was the question?" Rosamund flushed to the roots of her hair under the stern gaze of her mother.

Queen Adele chuckled. "Were you someplace else, dear? You looked lost in thought."

"Oh," she breathed. "I suppose I was."

"I asked if you gave any thought to what your gown might look like," the queen asked.

"Ah..." Brows drawn together, she looked to her mother who lifted a brow, clearly expecting an answer. "I haven't actually. All of this happened so suddenly."

Her mother frowned. But Adele was sympathetic.

"Yes, I suppose it did. Since you had no knowledge of the betrothal until today."

For a moment, Rosamund thought she could be friends with the queen. Her mother's frown deepened at Queen Adele's response. Though the woman didn't cut her mother a knowing, accusatory glance, her tone said it all.

Her father cleared his throat loudly. "I do realize what an error in judgement it was to keep it from you, Rosamund, but we thought it was for the best."

"For the best for you?" she fired.

Her mother continued to glare and frown.

"It was likely due to the Fae Royals—" Reginald began.

"That's enough, Reginald," Adele interrupted.

Rosamund's brows drew together in question. "What about the Fae royals?"

"They were guests at your christening," her father said, his gaze firmly planted on his plate.

Her mother signaled the servants and changed the subject. "How about dessert?"

But Rosamund was confused. She had never heard this about her christening. Certainly, she knew the nobility had come, but the Fae royals?

"Why did they come?" she asked, peering down the table at her father.

He was busy sawing through a piece of beef tenderloin. "I invited them." As he said this, he stabbed the meat with his fork and popped it into his mouth.

"I think that's enough of that talk," her mother said.

The servants arrived to clear away the dinner dishes. Her father looked forlorn when they took his plate away with the half-eaten tenderloin. In its place, they placed a dessert plate with a large slab of cake on it.

When they placed the cake in front of Rosamund, though, she merely stared at it. Her mouth had gone dry and she'd lost her appetite.

"I'm not hungry anymore," she said, then lifted her gaze to her mother. "May I be excused?"

Her mother said nothing for along moment as she considered her request.

"I'm very tired," Rosamund added.

Finally, her mother nodded. "Very well."

She pushed from the table and placed her napkin in her chair. The exit to the dining room seemed so far away and it took everything in her not to bolt into a run. Instead, she kept her hands by her side and took perfect, slow steps toward the door. Finally at the door, she pushed it open and slipped out.

But as she did so, she heard Queen Adele say, "Poor thing. I daresay it was a bit of a shock."

Rosamund skittered away from the door. While she wanted to stay and eavesdrop, she had other tasks to tend. She hurried away from the dining hall and headed for the kitchen. She knew there were servants hard at work, including the cook, but she hoped she could slip in and out unnoticed.

At the doorway, she paused, listening to the cacophony. Voices chattering, dishes clattering, water sloshing. The smell of roasted meat and vegetables wafted to her—remnants of their dinner. She peered around the corner. Most everyone was busy with their own tasks.

She spied a basket of fruit on the far counter. That would work. Next to that, half a loaf of bread. That would work, too.

Stepping into the kitchen, she worked her way down the long wall, past the open oven and to the counter. She snatched the basket off the counter, then reached for the loaf. But she paused, glancing at the bustling kitchen.

No one noticed her.

She grabbed the loaf and tucked it into the basket. Another quick glance around and she spied a discarded kitchen towel that looked relatively clean. She snagged it and threw it over the basket to cover the stolen property.

Then she inched her way back out of the kitchen. At the door, she was home free. She hurried out and then dashed down the long hallway, her heart ramming hard in her chest and her breathing rapid.

She'd done it! So far, her plan was working out.

Next, she had to find Lucy's room. She continued down the long corridor, going deeper into the castle than she'd ever been. She wasn't all that familiar with the servant's area, but she had a general idea of where Lucy's room was. Voices made her halt in the corridor. She pressed her back against the cold stone wall, her heart in her throat as her breath came in quick pants. She dared not breathe.

"Good night, Mrs. Peeler." It was Lucy's voice.

The girl must be heading up to help her change since she assumed dinner was over or close to over. Rosamund held her breath and waited until at last the girl came into view and headed down the hallway.

Right for her.

Her gaze immediately landed on her and she halted, peering at her in surprise. Her mouth formed a silent O.

"Princess?" she asked, her voice a rough whisper. "Was there something you needed?"

"Ah…" Rosamund remained in place, her back against the wall. Her hands started to shake.

Lucy's gaze flickered to the basket she held, then back up to her face. She frowned, question evident on her face as she tried to puzzle out why the princess loitered in the servant's wing holding a basket of food.

"Are you lost?" the girl asked.

"No," Rosamund said, finally finding her voice. "I need your help."

"My help?" She drew up taller as she gazed at her, perplexed. "Of course, princess. Whatever you need."

She almost snorted. When Lucy discovered what she needed, she may not be so ready to help. "Where is your room?"

Again, she gave her a confused look and then pointed. "Just there."

It was only a few steps away. "Let's go in there and I'll tell you what I need." She motioned for her to lead the way.

Lucy did and Rosamund fell in step behind her. The girl stopped at the first door and pushed it open, then stood aside for Rosamund to enter. The room was tiny and sparsely furnished, not at all the lavish suite she lived in. There was one narrow, lumpy bed with a few blankets and a pillow. A well-worn book rested on the middle of the bed. The mattress looked to be straw, not feather like hers. A table was next to the bed with a candleholder and one long taper that was lit to give the room a faint, warm glow. On the other side, a chamber pot and a small wardrobe that likely held the girl's clothes.

"You live here?" she asked, unable to hide her surprise.

"Yes, your highness." Lucy blushed, her cheeks turning a pale pink as she followed her in and closed the door.

The room was so small. So stuffy. And no window. How did she live like this?

"It's not as lavish as your suite, of course," the girl said, apologetic. "How can I help you?"

Rosamund stood a long moment in the center of the room, taking it all in. "Do all the servants live in rooms like this?"

"Most of us," she said. "Except for the ones who have more seniority. Their rooms are a bit bigger."

Rosamund thought of the scullery maid that had the worst job of all. Emptying chamber pots and scrubbing floors, the stove, pots and pans and cleaning vegetables, plucking chickens and scaling fish. Lucy, however, didn't have a physical job like that. She was allowed to dress her in her fine gowns and style her hair. If she left the castle and her life of luxury behind, would she end up as a servant in someone's household?

"Your highness?" Lucy asked. "You said you needed my help?"

She shook herself out of her thoughts. "Yes, I did, and well, perhaps I was wrong."

She peered at the small wardrobe, wondering how many gowns the girl had. Certainly not nearly the number she had in her wardrobe. Gowns for every day and every occasion. She couldn't bring herself to take one of the girl's gowns. She'd just have to find something else to wear.

"Shall I accompany you back to your room and help you prepare for bed?" the girl asked.

"No," Rosamund said, too quickly. "I can handle it myself."

Lucy was clearly baffled by her strange behavior. She eyed the basket again on her arm. "Are you certain? The laces on your dress—"

"Oh! Of course." Rosamund flushed. There was no way she would be able to remove the dress herself. She'd definitely need help.

"If I may ask, your highness, why do you have a basket on your arm?"

Feeling foolish, she uncovered the fruit and the bread. Lucy peered down at the basket, then glanced back up her. The surprise was evident on her face followed by question. Rosamund blew out a breath.

"This is just for later. Sometimes I get hungry in the night," she lied.

Lucy looked as though she didn't believe her, but said nothing. "I see."

"Why don't you walk me to my room?" she said, suddenly, trying to change the subject. "You can help me prepare for bed."

Still, she did not have suitable clothing for sneaking out into the night, but she'd worry about that later. She hooked her arm in Lucy's, plastered on her best smile, and together, they left and headed to her chamber.

Chapter 7

As soon as Lucy left, Rosamund hopped out of bed and paced, her mind racing. She'd placed the basket beside the door as they entered. Lucy eyed it as she left but said nothing more about it.

All she knew was she couldn't leave the castle in her nightgown. She hurried to her wardrobe and flung open the doors, peering at the array of gowns inside. Below, her shoes lined up in perfect order. She huffed out a breath. None of these would do. Perhaps, though, she could pick a day dress and then find something more suitable in one of the local villages.

She pushed through the gowns until she found a simple one in white with pale yellow daisies. She quickly dressed, struggling with the laces in the back by contorting her arms in awkward positions. But she succeeded. Then she grabbed her cloak from the peg near the door and flung it around her shoulders, pulling up the hood. Next, she grabbed the basket.

A momentary pause as she stood in the middle of her room, glancing around. Her heart pounded hard as she considered what she was about to do. A surge of determination ignited within her casting aside her doubt and fears. She was not going to back out now.

But she also knew she couldn't walk through the front door. Steeling her nerves, she headed for the balcony door and flung it open. The crisp spring air greeted her as well as the sound of crickets. She walked onto the balcony and peered down at the ground. It was too far down and there was no way to scale the wall with the basket on her arm.

She backed away, closing the door. She tapped her forefinger against her chin, thinking.

Perhaps there was another way. There was a postern gate at the back of the castle. Though they had never used it, she knew it was there in case they had ever come under siege and they needed a quick escape.

She stepped to her door and cracked it open, peering into the hall. It was empty. She slipped out of her room, hoping her parents were sleeping by now. Closing the door behind her with a soft snick, she hurried down the hall.

She made her way down the staircase, crossed the great hall to the door. With her heart beating in her throat, she pulled it open and stepped into the night. The air was crisp and cool but with spring undertones that promised a warm summer. Closing the door, she hurried across the courtyard. The stables were positioned by the gate and she halted there, considering taking a horse. That would raise more questions. Then again, did she really want to leave on foot?

She'd have to saddle her own horse, but it was something she knew how to do. With her heart in her throat, she entered the stables.

She heard the soft whicker of one of the horses. Hers was in the stall on the end. After she'd saddled it, she realized the basket was too cumbersome, so she removed the contents and wrapped everything in the cloth. One of the apples wouldn't fit. Her mare nudged her, then snorted. She giggled and held it out to her.

She chomped it in one bite. She patted the horse's neck, trying to calm her own nerves. It wasn't too late to turn back.

"I must be crazy," she whispered.

The mare responded with a soft whicker, as though she understood and were trying to give her encouragement.

"I have to go, don't I?" she asked.

The mare nudged her, looking for another treat and had no answer.

"Yes, I do," she said, trying to sound confident.

Then she stuck the wrapped food into the saddle bag.

Rosamund guided her horse out of the stall and into the night. The gate was nearby. It was closed. She led the horse to it. Her nerves were on edge as she approached it, peered at it and hoped there was a way to open it.

She needn't have worried. There was no lock. Merely a latch to keep it closed. She pulled it open and gazed into the night. There was a stone path that led away from the castle. With a gentle tug of the reins, she pulled along her horse and went through the gate. She paused only a moment to turn and close it.

And then she and her horse continued down the narrow stone path into the night.

Toward freedom.

In Woodhaven, Prince Phillip arrived back home with Charles and Jeffrey in tow. They relinquished their horses to the stable hand and then entered the keep. Phillip was tired and saddle sore from riding so hard to return home. Jeffrey was relentless. He'd made a promise to his mother to get him to Myst Hall in a few days' time and it was clear he intended to keep that promise.

"Get some rest. We leave at first light," Jeffrey said.

Charles was happy to join them on their travels, too. Phillip scowled.

He trudged up the stairs to his room and slammed the door, leaning against it.

Despite his fatigue, he pushed away from the door and entered his bedchamber. He discarded his dirty riding clothes and changed into clean breeches, tunic, padded vest. Then he pulled on his boots once more. He strapped his sword to his side as well as his favorite dagger on his other hip.

He took one last look around, as though bidding it farewell, and then left his bedchamber. While Charles and Jeffrey slept the night away, he would have a head start. He wasted no time as he headed for the stable.

The stable hand had yet to remove the saddle from his horse. He approached with a smile and good humor.

"Ho there," he called.

The stable hand, a young boy not much older than thirteen, gave him a quizzical look. "Your highness?"

"No need to take care of my horse." He approached the stall and reached for the reins, leading the horse out.

"I thought you were leaving in the morning?" the boy asked.

"Change of plans." He flashed a bright smile. "Tell the others in the morning I rode on ahead."

"Of course, your highness."

Phillip mounted and trotted out of the stable. He had no destination in mind. Only that he knew he had to escape.

When he was through the portcullis, he kicked the horse into a gallop. He suspected his freedom wouldn't last long, but he was going to enjoy it while he could.

CHAPTER 8

Exhaustion settled into Rosamund's bones as she gripped the reins. She held on tight, trying hard not to nod off in the saddle. She'd rode all night and was desperate for rest but knew if she stopped this soon, it would increase her chances of being found.

She thought of her parents and wondered if her absence was discovered yet. As the sun lifted and broke the horizon, it seemed reasonable to think they would find her gone by now. It wasn't long before she approached the village, Briar Hill. It was the closest one to the castle.

People were just beginning to open their shops as she entered through the village gates. It was still early. Somewhere in the distance, a rooster crowed and a dog barked. She paused, still on horseback, as she took in the surroundings.

Shops lined the main thoroughfare with everything from a baker to a butcher to a candlestick maker. At the end of the street was an inn with a tavern. Next to that was a clothing shop. Beyond that, rows of houses for the villagers. She glanced down at her gown and wondered if there was some way to acquire different clothes.

Perhaps something more suitable and not befitting a princess. She needed to blend in, after all.

Unfortunately, she had no money. She didn't want to give up her identity to the clothing shop owner and promise payment when she had no intention of returning to her father to ask for gold.

At the very least, she needed to get out of the saddle and rest before continuing. She pulled to a halt outside the tavern and dismounted. She tied up her horse and peered up at the swaying dilapidated sign boasting the name *The Sleeping Dragon Inn* in faded green letters.

She pushed through the door and entered.

On one side of the large room was a fireplace. The hearth was dark and cold. On the other, a bar lined with tall stools. Scattered throughout the room were more tables and chairs. No one was about. The place was deserted.

That was fine by her. She took a seat near the cold hearth, grateful to be at rest and not riding.

A woman bustled from the back room humming a nameless tune carrying a large stack of firewood. She headed for the fireplace. Rosamund sat up straighter in her chair as the woman approached. She dropped the firewood by the hearth. She hadn't noticed Rosamund was there at all.

She watched the woman for a long moment as she stacked the firewood on the log rack, still humming. Rosamund thought she better make her presence known and cleared her throat loudly. The woman jumped and emitted a high-pitched squeak.

"Hello," Rosamund said.

She placed a hand over her chest and closed her eyes, inhaling deeply and then exhaling. "You gave me a fright! I dinna know anyone was here."

"I'm sorry," she said. "I didn't mean to scare you."

She resumed her task of building a fire. "Breakfast isn't ready yet but will be in a bit." When the fire started, she brushed the dirt from her hands and rose, turning to her. She placed her hands on her hips. "What can I fetch you?"

"Oh," she breathed, and shifted in her seat. "Nothing. I...don't have any money to pay. I just wanted to come in for a rest."

The woman peered at her, her stern eyes examining her closely. "A rest, you say?"

"I've been traveling all night."

"Hmm," was her only response. She bustled away, disappearing once more in the back room.

Rosamund rested her back on the chair and watched as the fire took off, the flames increasing ever so slightly. The woman returned with a tray and paused at her table. She placed the tray in front of her that had a bowl of porridge, a spoon, and a tankard of mead. Rosamund stared at it then up at the woman.

"But—"

"On the house," she said and then gave her a faint smile. "You look exhausted. Eat. Get your strength. Dinna worry about paying."

"I can't do that," she said.

"You can. I run the place. I insist." Again, she smiled.

"Thank you," she said, her voice a whisper.

She took the spoon and dug into the thick porridge. Despite the food in her saddle bag, it wasn't enough to sustain her. This would get her through to her next meal, whenever that was.

A few others trickled in from the outside, taking seats at the bar. The woman returned to bring them food and drink. Rosamund didn't miss her glancing her way as if to check on her. After serving a man at a nearby table, she paused next to hers and took the seat opposite her, which surprised her.

"So," the woman said. "Who are you running away from?"

Rosamund peered at her as shock trickled through her. "What makes you think that?"

She looked her over. "I've seen enough runaways in my time to recognize the signs."

Her mouth went dry. "What are the signs?"

"For starters, you have dark circles under your eyes," she said. "Second, your dress." She wagged a finger at her. "That's not fit for riding. Is it?"

Rosamund glanced down at the delicate gown with the pale-yellow daisies. She kept her eyes down. "No."

"So, what or who are you running from?" the woman asked again.

"My parents," she said at last.

"Ah, I see." She got to her feet. "Come with me."

Rosamund's head snapped up in her direction, question flickering through her. The woman waved her to follow.

"Well, come on."

She pushed back from the table and followed the woman with round hips and a kind face through the tavern to the back room. She led her past a kitchen to a narrow staircase. Up she went and still Rosamund followed. At the top of the stairs, she pushed open a door to reveal a small living area. Clearly the woman lived here.

"Have a seat."

She motioned to a lumpy chair near the one window with threadbare curtains while she disappeared through another doorway.

Rosamund sat in the chair, her hands in her lap as she waited with her heart in her throat. She peered out the grimy window but there wasn't much to see but the side of another building. The woman returned minutes later with an armload of clothes. She placed them on the nearby dining table that only had one chair.

"Do you live here?" Rosamund asked.

"I do." She sorted through the clothes, holding up certain pieces, then folding and putting them aside.

"Alone?" Rosamund asked.

The woman paused to look at her over her shoulder. "Yes."

Rosamund wondered what led her to this life. How did she end up as the tavern owner? The woman picked up a stack of neatly folded clothes and turned to face her. She held them out to her.

"Here. This will be better than that gown."

"I don't understand." Rosamund slowly rose from the chair, eyeing the clothes.

"Traveling clothes," she said, pushing them into her hands. "You can change in there." She pointed to the doorway.

"That's very kind of you," she said, gazing down at the material in her hands. "What's your name?"

"Anne," she said.

"Thank you, Anne."

She took the clothes and entered the room, which was the smallest bedroom she had ever seen. It had nothing but a narrow bed and one wardrobe in the corner. A large box was on the floor open. Inside, there were other pieces of clothing shoved around haphazardly. Rosamund closed the door behind her and placed the stack on the bed to examine them piece by piece.

The stack included a pair of tan breeches, an ivory tunic that tied at the neck with cuffs that buttoned at the wrist, a padded vest, a soft jacket in taupe, tall woolen socks. She gazed down at the items, then stuck out a foot to examine her black soft shoe. She wondered where she would find something more suitable, but then decided to worry about that later.

Rosamund slipped off her cloak and quickly changed, folding her day dress neatly. She kicked off her shoes. Scooping them up along with her dress and cloak, she opened the door. Anne sat in the lumpy chair waiting for her to emerge. When she did, she hopped to her feet.

She looked her over, as though inspecting her, then paused on her stockinged feet.

"Ah, boots."

Anne went to a narrow closet and flung open the door. She knelt, then rummaged around the bottom until she came up with a pair of worn black boots. She handed them to Rosamund.

"These used to be mine. I hope they fit you."

"Oh," she breathed, staring at the boots. "I shouldn't—"

"Take them. I insist. I don't have much use for them anymore."

Cradling her items in one arm, she reached for the boots. Anne removed the dress, cloak and her shoes and waved her to the nearby chair. Rosamund sat on the edge and pulled on first one boot, then the other.

"They fit," she said.

"Good." The woman smiled, pleased with her handiwork.

"But I don't understand. Why are you helping me?" Rosamund asked, looking up at the woman who still held her clothes.

"You appeared to need it," Anne said. "Someone helped me once. A long time ago. Seemed fitting to help you out."

Rosamund was touched and she vowed to never forget the kindness. Perhaps someday she would pay her back in kind. She got to her feet and reached for her things. Anne handed them over.

"Thank you for everything," she said.

"You're most welcome. Now you'll at least have some comfort while riding."

She nodded. "Well, I should be on my way."

"Take care, lady. I hope you find what you're looking for," she said.

Not knowing what she was looking for, she merely nodded and said, "So do I."

CHAPTER 9

In the far reaches of the realm of Faery in the Eternal Court, Rowena spent the long days of the last eighteen years waiting for the Myst Kingdom to announce the death of the princess. And though the girl's birthday was still a few days away, she was impatient to see to it the king and queen were properly punished for their slight.

While the other Court rulers return to their lives, Rowena harbored her ill feelings for King Stephan, letting them fester over time until they had almost consumed her. She thought about her curse every day since the day of the christening. Remembering the royals' horror-stricken faces kept her warm at night.

She paced the confines of her cavernous great hall, waiting for her messenger to return with news. She had dispatched him days ago, watching as he sifted away from her court. All the while, she had thoughts of what to do if her plan did not succeed.

Her guard appeared in the great hall, clearing his throat to get her attention.

"Your majesty, he has returned," he announced.

"Send him in at once." She didn't need an explanation as to who had returned.

The messenger, though, was already entering the hall before she finished. He was a young Fae who had the ability to sift through time and space. A strong Fae in which she had placed her faith.

"What news?" she asked, her hands clasped in front of her as she waited.

"First, I must tell you the royal rose garden was removed and all roses outlawed. No one is allowed to plant roses in any part of the kingdom," he said. "As decreed by the king."

Fury bloomed through her chest. "Indeed."

She resumed her pacing, clasping her hands behind her back. King Stephan thought he was a clever man to decree such a thing.

"I saw no signs of roses anywhere," the boy added.

"And the princess?"

"Her birthday is in a few days. They were planning a celebration followed by her wedding to the northern prince, Phillip. The princess, however, disappeared."

This caught her attention. Pleasure at the news bloomed through her. So, her spell worked. Turning herself into a dragonfly was a risk but it appeared her coercion succeeded. The princess left home at her urging. She halted her pacing to face him.

"Disappeared?" she asked in her most innocent, surprised tone, though she already knew the truth of it.

"She left under the cover of darkness with a horse from the royal stable. No one knows where she went. No one saw her leave. The king and queen are quite worried about her."

Rowena tapped her forefinger against her chin. "Interesting news indeed."

"There is more," he said.

"Pray continue."

"The king and queen from Woodhaven arrived without the prince," he said. "It was said he was to arrive a few days after them. He has yet to arrive."

"No prince or princess. Where, then, have they gone?"

"The prince travels southward," he said. "Toward the Mystwood Forest."

She lifted one dark brow. "How do you know this?"

"I turned myself into a crow and tracked him." He grinned, pleased with himself.

She, too, was pleased at the boy's resourcefulness. "And the princess?"

"She rides northward. It appears, my queen, they have both deserted their titles and their kingdoms."

"How very interesting," she muttered. She looked the young man over. "Tell me, what is your name?"

"Ferrin, my queen."

An idea rose and she finally had a way to get her revenge on King Stephan.

"Ferrin, you have done me a great service and shall be rewarded for your loyalty. I appoint you as one of my trusted advisors."

He bowed low. "Thank you, your majesty."

"Now, go. I will call upon you again when I have need of you."

He backed out of the room to do her biding. Rowena, though, needed to find a way to bring the prince and princess together. She returned to her chamber, where she consulted the green orb she used only in the most desperate times. The orb was small enough to fit in the palm of her hand and rested on a rosewood pedestal when not in use. It was called the All-Seeing Eye. It used much of her power and made her weak.

She cupped her hands around it. "Show me the prince of Woodhaven," she whispered.

It came alive a moment later with an image of the young prince riding south toward the forest.

"Show me the princess of Myst," she said.

The image switched to the girl riding north to the forest.

A smile curled her lips. With her hands still cupped around the orb, she began the incantation.

"By the threads of fate and paths unknown, weave a spell to entwine these two hearts over distance shown. Let their spirits align, bring their souls together in connection forever entwined."

Then she blew a breath into the orb, releasing the spell into their world. She dropped her hands and the orb went dark. Drained of her power and energy, she collapsed. But as things went dark for her, she smiled, triumphant.

Rosamund left the village behind, grateful for the help from Anne, and headed northward toward the forest. She wasn't sure where she was headed. She only knew she had to put as much distance between her and home as possible.

By nightfall, she made it to the boundary of the Mystwood Forest, the trees standing like tall, shadowy sentries. She halted her horse and peered up at them, a bit of apprehension trickling through her. She had never traveled without an escort, much less entered a forest alone. Was she certain she wanted to continue?

Turning back wasn't an option, though she did wonder how her parents were faring. Did they miss her? Worry about her? Wonder where she'd gone? Were they, even now, searching for her?

As she pondered all of this, something compelled her to continue into the forest. There was no explanation for it, but she had this overwhelming need to enter and find shelter for the night. She kept going.

The Mystwood Forest was so large, the border of the two kingdoms, Myst and Woodhaven, went through it. The northern edge was in Woodhaven, the southern in Myst. Thinking of the kingdom to the north made her think of Prince Phillip and her forced betrothal. She would decide in the morning which direction she would go, but it was not to be north into Woodhaven.

As she rode deeper into the forest, the shadows grew darker. Nocturnal creatures foraged in the underbrush while overhead, an owl hooted. She shifted in the saddle, straining her eyes to see into the darkness. For what, she didn't know.

The trees thinned and beyond there was a dark cabin in the glen. She headed there, pushing her horse into a quick trot. Once she arrived, she stepped down and held onto the reins, peering at the cabin with darkened windows. No smoke curled from the chimney. It appeared to be abandoned.

She tied the reins to the porch handrail, then removed the wrapped food from the saddle bag. She took a tentative step, the wood creaking under her weight. It seemed to hold, so she ascended the other two steps and paused at the door. A quick knock and then silence.

Reaching for the knob, she pushed open the door. It groaned as if from nonuse. She poked her head inside. Darkness greeted her.

"Hello?"

No answer. She took that as a good sign and pushed the door open the rest of the way. In the shadows, she saw the outlines of furniture. Beyond the small living area was a kitchen, dark and unwelcoming. A staircase was to her left leading up to what she supposed was a loft.

She stood there a long moment, trying to decide what to do next. She hadn't any way to light the lantern that hung by the door.

The faint sound of hooves caught her attention. She spun in the doorway and looked out, her heart beating a wild beat as she waited. Her breath pooled in her chest as she stared into the night wondering who was headed her way. Had her parents found her?

A lone rider came into view heading right for the cabin.

She stiffened and stepped back through the open door into the shadows. She dropped the wrapped food on a table in the small living area. Glancing around, she looked for a weapon. She found a poker by the fireplace and quickly dashed to it, taking up the iron bar and holding it aloft, ready to strike. The darkness concealed her as she stood still, watching and holding her breath.

The rider appeared to be a man. He halted his horse next to hers, peering at it and though she could not see his face, she assumed he was as confused as she. He dismounted, swinging his leg over the horse in a slow movement and dropped to the ground. He paused there, his hand on his hip, which she assumed was the hilt of his sword.

"Who's there?" he called.

Her heart rammed like a war drum against her chest as she remained in place.

"I seek shelter for the night," he called. "Nothing more."

Rosamund held the poker so tight, her hands cramped.

The mystery man held up his hands in surrender. "I mean no harm."

He sounded reasonable, but then, weren't most murderers and highwayman reasonable?

"Go away," she said. Her voice only shook a little.

He remained where he was. "I wish I could. I can't explain it, but I was compelled to this place. As though something led me here."

She stilled as she peered at him. She, too, was compelled to come here though she didn't know why or how.

"Who are you?" she asked from her concealed position.

"A mere traveler. Passing through and seeking a place to rest for the night." He paused, then, said, "Who are you?"

He sounded sincere. She relaxed her stance a bit but still held the makeshift weapon.

"How do I know I can trust you?" she demanded.

"How do I know I can trust *you*?" he countered.

Fair question.

"I mean you no harm," he continued. "I've been riding for a few days. I just want to rest."

She certainly understood that. "I've been riding for a few days, too. I want to rest, too."

"Then we understand each other." He took a step up on the porch.

"Stay where you are," she snapped, clutching the poker tighter.

He halted, his hands still held in surrender.

"Remove your weapon," she demanded.

He removed his sword belt and dropped it on the porch at his feet. Then he removed a dagger at his waist and dropped it next to his sword.

"I'm unarmed, my lady. Does that make you feel better?" There was a smile in his voice.

"I'm not unarmed. How does that make *you* feel?" she said.

"Safe."

Despite herself, she snickered. She dropped the poker to her side.

"Do you have matches?" she asked.

"Yes," he said.

"Come in and light the lantern by the door. When I see your face, then I will decide if you can stay."

He emitted a low chuckle. "As you say, my lady."

He moved inside the door, his hand in his pocket. A moment later, she heard the strike of a match followed by the flare of the flame. His face was illuminated by the yellow-orange flickering fire. He lit the lantern hanging by the door, then removed it from the bracket and held it aloft close to his face, brightening his features.

Her breath caught as she got her first glimpse of him. As soon as their eyes met, something happened between them she could not explain. As though a silvery thread connected them, pulling them together in a way she did not understand. She felt drawn to him.

He was handsome. The light from the lantern glinted off gold strands of his dark hair. His face was chiseled to perfection with a strong jaw. She wasn't sure of the color of his eyes. From what she could tell by the light, they were a rich honey color. He wore a cloak clasped at the throat with a silver pin. Beyond that, she couldn't see much else about his clothes.

"Does my face please you, my lady?"

His jest would have been funny if it hadn't been so close to the truth.

"You seem harmless enough," she said at last.

"Do I?" He smirked.

"You're a stranger to me," she said.

"True. However, that can be remedied with a simple introduction." Holding the lantern aloft, he asked, "What's your name, my lady?"

A good question. She wasn't prepared to give up her true identity. What if he were one of the castle guards in disguise? She wasn't ready to return.

"Rose," she said at last, shortening her name. No one had ever called her that.

"Well, Rose. It's lovely to make your acquaintance."

When he offered nothing more, she asked, "And you are?"

A smile lifted the corners of his mouth. "Edward, my lady. You may call me Edward."

Chapter 10

He didn't know why he decided to use his grandfather's name as an alias. It was the first name that popped into his head. He felt as though he needed to conceal his true identity as a prince until he knew more about the girl and who she was. As she didn't trust him, he didn't trust her.

She lowered the weapon she had clutched in her hand and relaxed her stance. "Well, then. You can come in, Edward."

He stepped through the doorway. As the circle of light from the lantern extended, he got his first glimpse of her. His heart tripped and his gut clenched as their eyes met. A shimmering light passed between them. He wondered if she sensed it, too. If she did, she gave no indication.

Her braided golden hair hung over one shoulder. She had a round face with perfect, full lips. The lantern light glinted off her skin, making it appear as though it shimmered. That seemed unlikely and he decided it was nothing more than his imagination.

It was her eyes that dazzled him. Emerald with gold flecks fringed in dark lashes. Something about the way she looked at him sent a shudder deep within him.

Tearing his gaze away from her, he glanced around the cabin. He stood in a shabby living area with old furniture covered in dust. A fireplace was on one wall. There was a kitchen and a wooden table and chairs beyond the living area. A staircase led up to the loft overhead.

She leaned the fire poker against the wall near the hearth.

He eyed the wrapped package on the table. "Is that food?"

"Just some bread and an apple." She moved to the table and picked it up, pushing off the cloth.

He stepped around her and placed the lantern on the table in the kitchen. It illuminated the room, showing off dust and cobwebs hanging from every corner. The fireplace had remnants of ash, indicating someone used it at some point in the past.

"I'll find some firewood and get a fire started."

Though he didn't know her, he felt it was his duty to build a fire to keep them warm. He headed back out to the woods, pausing to pick up his sword and dagger from the porch. He replaced them both on his person. It didn't take long to find enough wood to start a fire. When he returned, Rose was in the small kitchen washing plates.

"There's a well outside the back door," she said, sounding pleased.

As he started to build the fire, she busied herself with cutting the bread and placing the pieces on the plates. Next, she cut up the apple. She filled two cups with water and brought them over, handing him one. When the fire was going, he sat at the table. She handed him a plate and took the seat opposite him.

"It's not much," she said, sounding apologetic.

It made him smile. "It's perfect. Better than starving." He broke off a piece of bread and popped it into his mouth. It was a few days stale. "So, what is a girl like you doing out here?"

She fiddled with a torn piece of bread in front of her, a thoughtful expression on her pretty face. "Would you believe me if I told you I ran away from home?"

Phillip peered at her, amusement flickering through him. "You did? Why?"

She shifted in her seat as she contemplated her answer. "It's complicated." She granted him a weak smile.

"Isn't it always?" He chuckled.

"What about you? What are you doing out here?"

He sat back in the chair, holding a piece of the bread. "I'm looking for adventure."

"Adventure?" That seemed to pique her interest. She sat up straighter. "Where are you headed?"

"Wherever the wind takes me." He grinned. It was the best answer he had, because truly he didn't know.

She propped her elbow on the table, placed her chin in her hand, and emitted a gusty sigh. "I'd love a good adventure."

She sounded wistful and it made him smile. Indeed, it seemed he couldn't stop smiling around her. It also made him realize how different they were and wonder if it was truly safe for her to be traveling unguarded.

"Well, I'm headed north. I think," she added.

"You think?" North would lead her into Woodhaven, his kingdom.

"Maybe west." She shrugged one shoulder and gave him a broad grin. "Wherever the wind takes me."

That made him laugh.

There was something endearing and sweet about her. And yet, he sensed she really did want adventure. As though she wanted to be free. Perhaps that was why she ran away from home.

He related to that. He, too, wanted to be free from his life of court and politics. To spend his days hunting and hawking and drinking instead of running a kingdom and...marrying that princess he was supposed to marry.

He thought of the princess and his parents at Myst Hall and wondered if they were missing him. He thought of Charles and Jeffrey and wondered if they were searching for him when they realized he'd stolen into the night like a thief.

"Why did you run away from home?" he asked, peering at her from across the table.

She kept her eyes downcast on the decimated bread before her. She lifted one shoulder in a half shrug. "I doubt you would understand."

"Try me," he said in an inviting tone. "I'd really like to know."

She looked up at him through her lashes and his heart stuttered. Such a strange reaction to this girl he just met.

"Really?"

"Yes, really."

"I wanted a different life than the one my parents wanted for me," she said at last.

There was something cryptic about the way she said it. As though she were telling him enough truth to appease him. Whatever the reason, she wanted to keep it to herself.

It was yet another thing he related to.

"I feel as though we are kindred spirits," he said.

Rose tilted her head to one side. "How so?"

"I, too, want a different life than the one my parents have planned for me."

She stared at him a long moment in silence, then gave a little nod. "Then we appear to understand each other."

"We do."

She ate another piece of bread, then the apple pieces, and washed it all down with the small cup of water. She fought off a yawn. She had deep circles under her eyes as though she hadn't slept.

"It will be light soon," he said. "We should rest. You take the loft. I'll sleep in the chair."

She glanced at the old chair with the frayed upholstery. She frowned, a look of disgust flickering over her face. "In that old thing?"

He saw it was covered in a thick layer of dust. "I'll clean it before I go to sleep."

Rose stood, taking their plates and cups away to the small kitchen and placing them on the counter. He noticed she had only eaten a few bites of the bread. Why did he have a sudden urge to make sure she was cared for?

"I'm sure the loft isn't much better." As she turned to face him, she caught him staring at her.

Their eyes met again. Deep in her emerald depths, he saw strength and an independent spirit unable to be denied. He saw a wild heart that sought adventure and freedom. He saw a girl who had a thirst for a life she had not yet lived. While he did and lived as he pleased.

Her cheeks warmed. A breath shuddered out of her. He tore his gaze away and turned to the fire, stoking it to keep the flames going and pretending she was nothing but a girl he happened upon. In an abandoned cabin. In the woods. And she was alone.

"I'll, um, see what's in the loft," she said at last, clearly affected by the way he looked at her.

She skittered past him and hurried up the steps, her footfalls loud on the stairs as she made her way to the loft.

What was wrong with him? He had never been so affected by a girl before. He sensed Rose was different. Rose was special. Rose needed to be traveling with an escort west through the forest. An overwhelming urge to protect her shifted through him. In the morning, he would ask her to ride with him.

He heard rustling overhead and stood, glancing upward and wondering if she needed help. Then a thud followed by a muffled, feminine *oof*. Then more rustling. What was she doing up there?

A moment later, she bounded down the stairs with an armload of fabric, a bright smile on her face.

"Look what I found!" In her arms were blankets and a pillow. "Clean linens."

She pushed them into his arms. He had no choice but to take them.

"The nights are still chilly," she said. "You'll want a blanket or two."

He stared down at the woolen blanket, the feather pillow, and his heart melted a little. Then he glanced back at her. Her cheeks were still pink but this time from exertion.

"What about you?" he asked.

"The mattress is lumpy but it'll do. I found more blankets and a pillow. I'll be fine." She looked at the dusty chair with dismay. "Are you sure about that?"

"Well, since there's nothing else..."

She marched over to the chair and surveyed it, her hands on her hips. Then she pulled the seat cushion off and smacked it with her hand. A cloud of dust plumed. She sneezed. They exchanged a look, then a laugh. She dropped it on the floor and spun around, looking at the remaining furniture.

The sofa had seen better days. The seat cushions were leaking stuffing. But there were seat back pillows worth saving. She grabbed them all and trotted over, dropping them on the floor by the fire, creating a make-shift bed.

"How's that?" she asked. "Better than that old chair."

He was awestruck by her caring and consideration. "It's wonderful."

Rose reached for the blankets she'd given him, taking them back. She took one and spread it over the three cushions. Then placed the feather pillow on one end. Finally, the second blanket she folded neatly and laid at the foot. A tidy little bed by the fire.

"That should keep you warm, especially by the fire."

She brushed nonexistent dust from her hands. When their eyes met once again, it was difficult to ignore the warmth spreading through him and his quickened heartbeat. Here was this girl who had shared her bread and apple with him and made him a bed by the fire. She was adorable.

"Thank you," he said.

"You're welcome." As she said it, her cheeks turned pink again. "Good night!"

And then she bounded up the stairs to the loft. He stood a moment, letting his racing pulse slow to normal as he sank to the floor. He removed his sword and dagger and placed them on the floor, then removed his boots.

He stretched out on the cushions, his feet dangling over the edge, then pulled up the blanket to cover himself. He watched the flickering flames of the fire and came to a decision.

In the morning, he was definitely going to encourage her to travel with him.

CHAPTER 11

Rosamund sprinted up to the loft, her booted feet clumping on the wood steps. Her heart pounded in concert with her steps. When she made it to the top, she halted, her breath see-sawing in and out. Her hands shook.

What was she doing? Was she out of her mind?

She cast a quick look at the carnage she'd left behind to take him blankets and a pillow. The wardrobe in the corner stood open, the contents haphazardly tossed about as she looked for something to take to him. If only to speak to him again.

She was right about one thing. His eyes *were* the color of honey with such depth and emotion that it made her pulse skitter. She had never seen eyes that color before.

The way he looked at her made her heart sing. She didn't know why she couldn't bear the thought of him sleeping in that rickety old chair. But something deep inside her made her want to make sure he was comfortable. Her mind went into action as she pulled off the cushions and placed them by the fire.

When she glanced at him, he had an amused look on his face that switched to adoration. She shoved that thought aside, unable to believe he had such a thought about her.

She pulled the dusty coverlet off the bed and dropped it on the floor at the foot. Then she made her bed. In the wardrobe, she found more clean blankets and pillows. She fluffed the pillows and then sat on the bed, pulling off her boots. She sat a moment, thinking of the kind woman, Anne, and how she had helped her.

Not for the first time, she wondered if her father had sent his men to look for her. She found it unlikely that he wouldn't, given she was his only daughter and princess.

She laid back on the bed and glanced at the one widow. Grime covered the surface, but she was still able to see the outline of trees. As she curled on her side, she wondered where she would go tomorrow. She and Edward would go their separate ways. Would she ever see him again? A sudden pang of longing went through her at the thought of never seeing him again. As she drifted off to sleep, she decided it was for the best.

The following morning, the first twitter of birds woke her. Sunlight illuminated the dirty window, waking her from her restless sleep. She laid there a long moment, listening to the sounds outside the cabin and straining her ears for any movement downstairs.

She heard nothing. It was silent.

Had he left?

She sat straight up, still listening and hearing nothing. Shoving off the blanket, she hurried down the stairs in her stocking feet and halted at the bottom. His cushions and blankets were still on the floor by the fireplace. Only embers remained in the hearth. The cabin door stood open, letting in the fresh morning breeze that still had a chill to it. She peered outside to see both their horses still tied up.

Then she heard the faint whistling of a tune she didn't recognize. She waited until he came into view, carrying a bucket of water. She watched as he watered first his horse, talking to it in a low voice and patting the neck, and then hers. He went to his saddlebag and rummaged through it, bringing out a couple of apples. He fed both horses.

Her heart fluttered at the way he cared for the two animals.

When he was finished, he whistled again and then ascended the porch steps, the bucket still in his hand. He stopped whistling and halted when he saw her.

"Oh, good morrow," he said and grinned. He held up the bucket. "You were right about the water."

"You're up early," she said and realized it was the silliest thing to say.

"Couldn't sleep."

She glanced at the cushions still on the floor. "Was it not comfortable?"

"The cushions were fine." He moved into the cabin, dropping the bucket on the table. "It seems I couldn't turn off my mind."

His gaze landed on hers, making her pulse quicken.

"How did you sleep?" he asked.

"The bed was lumpy but otherwise fine."

An awkward silence descended between them. She backed toward the stairs. "I forgot my boots."

Then she was up them in a sprint. At the top, she pressed her hand against her raging heart and closed her eyes, trying to calm her nerves. Her reaction to him was ridiculous. He was just a man, nothing more.

A very handsome man with an engaging smile and gorgeous eyes.

Now that it was light out, she noticed his clothes were fine which told her he was more than a peasant. Was he part of the nobility? And since they met in the forest that straddled both the Myst Kingdom and Woodhaven Kingdom, she wondered where he hailed from.

It was too early in their relationship to ask and, she told herself, it didn't matter. She was never going to see him again.

She bent and picked up her boots, then sat on the bed to pull them on. Her cloak was draped over the end of the bed. She grabbed it as she headed back down the stairs. In the living room, she saw him replacing the cushions. He'd already folded the blankets and left them on the kitchen table in a neat pile.

Who was this guy?

He turned to her when she entered, a contemplative look on his face.

"I was thinking," he said, choosing his words slowly. "I'm heading west through the forest. If you're heading that way, too, it seems to me the two of us could travel together."

She stared at him in utter shock, surprised at the unexpected offer. He had not mentioned going west last night. Had he decided to go that way since that was her named destination?

Before refusing, she heard herself say, "I would like that."

"Great. I'll be outside." He motioned to the open doorway, then headed out.

Rosamund wrapped the cloak around her shoulders and hoped she wasn't about to make a mistake. She left the cabin, closing the door behind her.

When she emerged, he stuck his foot in the stirrup and mounted. She walked to the other side of hers and did the same.

"Now," he said, cutting her a glance with a mischievous gleam in his eyes. "Let's go find that adventure."

Together, they turned their horses from the cabin and started down the shadowy path.

Rowena watched through the All-Seeing Eye to see her plan worked. The two had come together and now appeared to be traveling together. Now, to make sure the curse she placed on the princess all those long years ago would at last be fulfilled. She had the perfect plan for that.

CHAPTER 12

Rosamund tried to ignore her rumbling stomach, but it was difficult when it was making so much noise. The meager pieces of bread and apple she had the night before were not enough and she was out of apples. Her only hope was that Edward didn't hear.

As they continued on in amicable silence, he cut her a glance. A wisp of a smile was on his face. Something told her he heard her growling stomach even with the distance between them.

"You know," he said, "there's a town not far from here. We could be there by midday and have a meal before continuing on."

A heated flush crawled up her neck to her cheeks.

"Is it that obvious?" she asked, sheepish.

He laughed. "Truthfully, I'm famished, too. I've never been one to miss a meal." He gave her a sideways grin.

"Nor I," she said and then laughed. It was funny how much alike they seemed to be. From his clothes to his mannerisms, she suspected he was part of the nobility. But the question was from which kingdom? Hers or Woodhaven?

She didn't know all the nobles in Myst, so it seemed reasonable he could be from there.

"What do you say? Shall we?" he asked.

She nodded. "That would be nice."

He veered his horse to the right to head north. She did the same. But as they headed toward the forest, they heard the thunder of hooves behind them. She glanced back but saw nothing. Even so, her heart picked up speed. It sounded like more than one horse, which alarmed her.

"Do you hear that?" Her voice was a roughened whisper.

"Horses? Sounds like they're behind us." He seemed unconcerned.

But Rosamund had a knot of fear deep in her gut. She clutched the reins so tight, her hands cramped. She cast a swift glance back over her shoulder again and saw the four riders charging down the path. They were all dressed in full plate armor. One carried the sigil of Myst Hall.

She emitted a strangled gasp.

"What is it?" he asked, glancing at her with concern.

"I think we should hurry."

She kicked her horse into a gallop, not really knowing where they were going. She dashed through the trees, leaning down close to her horse as she steered the mare through the dense vegetation.

"Rose, wait!" he called.

But she didn't have time to wait. Those were her father's soldiers. They were no doubt looking for her to bring her back to the castle. The last thing she wanted was for that to happen in front of Edward.

The thunder of hooves behind her told her he'd caught up to her. Even so, she pushed her horse harder and faster, heading for the tree line in her sights. All she had in mind was getting out of the forest and into the town he mentioned. Perhaps there she would be able to blend in for a bit.

"Rose," he called. "Slow down."

She said nothing as she continued on her way, her focus dead ahead.

Finally, he pulled up next to her, reaching for her reins. "Slow down."

Much to her dismay, he slowed her horse to a trot.

"What was that about?" he asked, confusion etched on his face.

She sat straight and tall in the saddle, her mind racing to come up with an excuse. "I thought those men were chasing us."

A ridiculous excuse, but hopefully he'd buy it.

"Those men back there?" He nodded behind them. "They looked like soldiers from Myst Hall."

Exactly why she didn't want to get caught. A breath shuddered out of her. "Did they?"

"Yes, they did." His gaze narrowed as he looked her over. Suspicion laced his tone.

Her nerves jangled. She kept her eyes forward so her expression wouldn't give her away. She didn't hear the sound of the men behind them, so she hoped they had put enough distance between them and left them far behind.

"How close is this town you mentioned?" she asked, trying to make it sound as if it were nothing more than an innocent question.

"Westcliff is just outside the forest," he said.

"Good." She gave him a bright smile. "I'm ravenous!"

Luck was on their side. True to his word, they arrived in Westcliff around midday. By then, her hunger pains had become almost unbearable. She was lightheaded to the point of fainting.

But she managed to ride on as they entered the bustling town through the gates on the southside. Westcliff was part of the kingdom of Woodhaven near the southern border near the boundary of the Mystwood Forest.

It was larger than she expected. The main thoroughfare was lined with buildings. At the end of the main street, the church. Beyond that, more streets that hosted thatched roof huts for residences. And beyond the streets, fields and gardens where the residents grew their crops and grazed their animals.

Edward seemed to know where he was headed as he trotted down the narrow main street which was jammed with people, horses, and carts. She spotted a black cat darting through the crowd.

She followed, keeping her reins tight as her head swiveled from side to side, taking it all in. This was not like Briar Hill, where she stopped at the tavern and the kind woman, Anne, reclothed her.

No, this was much bigger. The buildings, she realized, were businesses. Everything from a dressmaker, to a candlemaker, to a baker, to a smithy. There was a shop for weapons, an apothecary, even a cobbler. The smell of refuse reached her and she frowned, trying hard not to gag.

He saw her expression and chuckled. "The tavern is just there." He pointed ahead.

She nodded and followed him through the narrow street to the tavern, where he tied up his horse. She dismounted and did the same, glad to be out of the saddle. Glad, too, for the bustle of the town and hoped it would keep her concealed. She also hoped the soldiers had decided to go another way and not follow them out of the forest.

The faded sign over the tavern read *The Red Lion* and a picture of a roaring lion underneath it. Edward headed for the door, then paused to see her staring up at the sign.

"Is there something wrong?" he asked.

She shook her head. "Not at all." Then gave him a reassuring smile.

She followed him through the door into the rowdy tavern. The place was full. A bar lined one wall with every stool occupied. He led her through to the back, where one table was open. There he took a seat against the wall, positioning himself so he could watch the door. She took the seat next to him rather than across from him. There, she, too, would be able to watch the door in case the soldiers ended up here looking for her.

Moments after they sat, the tavern maid bustled up to their table. Her gown was old and stained. Her face, haggard and her eyes tired. Her dark hair was pulled back from her face with sprigs sprouting from what was once her perfect coif. She plopped down dark bread and two tankards of ales.

"What'll it be?" she said, her tone impatient.

He eyed the bread in front of them, then glanced up at her with his best winning smile. "Beef stew for both of us."

Nodding, she hurried off, her hips swaying as she went. Rosamund sat straight in her chair, her hands in her lap, as she eyed the door. As though waiting for the soldiers to find her and take her back.

"How did you know about this place?" she asked.

"I've been here before," he said.

"You have?"

He nodded. "Only once. When I was returning home after a hunting trip."

"So, you hunt?" She gave him a sideways glance.

"Sometimes."

She noticed he, too, kept his gaze on the door. He seemed to be on edge, like her. Perhaps seeing the soldiers had spooked him as well.

"What do you hunt?" She was making small talk, she knew, and was merely trying to keep the conversation alive.

"Wild boar. Sometimes pheasant. Sometimes deer."

"Oh," the word shuddered out of her.

He leaned toward her then and dropped his voice. "Do you want to know a secret?"

She nodded.

"I don't really hunt." His face lit up in a wide smile.

"What do you do then?" she wanted to know.

"Sit in taverns and drink ale with my friends."

With a twinkle in his eye and a sly smile playing on his lips, he exuded an irresistible charm that made it impossible not to be drawn into the mischievous energy surrounding him. Delight shifted through her as a soft chuckle escaped her lips, her fingers wrapping around the handle of the tankard with a sense of contentment.

"You don't actually kill anything?" she asked.

He shook his head. "Never. Sometimes we camp under the stars and pretend we're going to hunt at dawn. But we never do."

"Camping under the stars sounds nice." Her tone was wistful as she thought about the freedom he had.

She picked up the tankard and sniffed the ale. It smelled sour but she took a healthy swig anyway. The taste was awful as she swallowed it, then immediately grabbed the bread and tore off a hunk. She popped it into her mouth.

Edward chuckled. "Not used to drinking ale, are you?"

"I've never had ale." It was an admission she didn't want to make.

In her many formal dinners, she'd had wine certainly. But never the dark, heady ale or whiskey her father seemed to enjoy. After their dinners, the men went off to their own sitting room to smoke cigars and drink more ale while the ladies spent the evening in silence either reading or sewing.

Thinking of that now bored her.

She took another swig of ale as the beef stew arrived. The tavern maid dropped two large bowls on the table in front of them, then scurried off to take care of more patrons.

Rosamund peered down at the thick stew with chunks of beef, carrots, and potatoes. Her mouth watered. She took up the spoon and dug in with alacrity. When she'd polished off the bowl, she sat back in the chair with a sigh of contentment. Then realized he was only halfway through his.

A wave of scorching heat pounded through her, piercing her cheeks.

He laughed.

"I see the beef stew was good," he said.

As she was about to answer, the door to the tavern flung open. Four soldiers in armor stormed in. She sat a little straighter in her chair, her contentment wiped away and replaced with a stabbing fear. These had to be the men she saw on the trail behind them. They had caught up and now they were here looking for her.

She pulled her hood up and slunk down in her chair.

Edward, meanwhile, noticed the men and gave her a sideways glance as she tried to hide under the material of the hood.

He dropped his spoon. "Are they looking for you?"

She merely shook her head, keeping her eye on the men who spoke with the man behind the bar. Thankfully, they hadn't talked to him when they arrived. She hoped to hide in the corner of the shadows. But then the man who appeared to be the leader turned from the bar and scanned the large room, his eyes alighting on each patron.

When he spotted them, he started their way. Edward scooted closer to her.

"They are, aren't they?" He kept his voice low.

"I fear they are." She dropped her gaze to her hands in her lap.

The soldier stopped at their table, his hand on the hilt of his sword. Rosamund stole a glance upward to see him scrutinizing both of them. He was not one of the guards she knew. For that, she was grateful. Edward, meanwhile, leaned back in his chair as though the sight of the man didn't bother him at all.

"We're looking for a woman. Tall with blonde hair and green eyes," the soldier said.

"I'm looking for a woman, too," he snapped back. "Though I confess I haven't found one worthy."

The man scowled at him, then looked at Rosamund. "Perhaps you've seen her." It was a question directed to her. "She would have left Myst a few days ago."

Edward threw his arm around the back of her chair. "My sister and I are traveling through town. We haven't seen anyone. Especially someone from Myst."

The guard's eyes narrowed. "What's that supposed to mean?"

"Only that those of us from Woodhaven prefer not to fraternize with those from Myst."

Rosamund shifted in her seat as she cut him a glance. He continued to look at the soldier with guarded eyes and she understood then it was all a ruse. The guard's eyes landed on her then.

"This is your sister, eh?" He sounded unconvinced. "What's your name, girl?"

"I'm afraid she can't answer you. She's mute," Edward said.

It took everything in her to remain perfectly still and not snap her head in his direction. The guard bent down to give her a closer inspection. She stared back, keeping her gaze strong and sure as he peered at her with black suspicious eyes.

"You have green eyes," the man said.

"A gift from my mother," Edward said, sounding jovial. "I can assure you this girl isn't the one you seek. We traveled together down from Dundeen. She hasn't left my sight."

The soldier straightened, his hand still on the hilt of his sword. He did not appear to believe Edward's story. He lingered there a moment longer, glancing between the two of them, and then turned and headed back to the front of the tavern.

The other three had fanned out through the crowd, asking questions and looking for her. When they finally all left, she blew out a breath. Edward dropped his arm and scooted back to his previous position.

"Perhaps, Rose, you tell me why a soldier of Myst Hall was looking for you." He turned to face her, his eyes piercing through her. "And who you really are."

CHAPTER 13

Phillip threw coins on the table to pay for their meal and then rose, his chair scraping back with a loud screech. The fear on Rose's face told him everything he needed to know. She was the girl the soldiers from Myst Hall were looking for. Likely the ones who were in the forest not far behind them and why she insisted on galloping away from them.

But who was she and why would she be running from them?

Her face had drained of color as she rose from the chair. She followed him out of the tavern and into the late afternoon sunshine where he turned to her and gripped her by the elbow.

"Who are you?" he repeated. "Are you a thief?"

Her eyes flew open. "No!"

"Then what did you do to garner the attention of four soldiers from Myst Hall?" His voice was demanding, terse.

"How do you know they were from Myst Hall?"

She blinked owlish eyes. He thought for certain he saw the palpitation of her pulse in the long column of her neck. He gave her a deadpan look.

"I recognized the sigil on his cloak."

A look of discomfort flickered over her face, as though she, too, had noticed the sigil from Myst Hall. She shifted her weight from one foot the other and tried to dislodge her arm from his grip, but he held fast. It confirmed his thoughts that she was the one they were looking for. Yet he was compelled to lie to them. Why, he did not know.

"You told them I was your mute sister," she pointed out. "Why did you do that?"

He tipped his head to one side. "You looked frightened. I was trying to help you."

Confusion trickled over her face then realization when his words sunk in. She flushed, her cheeks turning pink which, if it were under any other circumstance, might be adorable.

He released her and walked to the side of his horse. He shouldn't have covered for her. He should have let them take her. Now, he was an accomplice to keeping her out of the soldier's hands.

"I thank you for that," she said. "And I promise I'm not a thief, nor have I done anything nefarious."

He was still unconvinced. "Then why do they want you?"

She pressed her lips together into a thin line, as though she wanted to tell him the truth but couldn't. As though the truth would be damaging. If she was hunted by the soldiers, then she must have done something to garner their attention. Attention he could not afford.

If they captured her, they would likely capture him and the last place he wanted to be was Myst Hall. Where his irate parents were likely still visiting. Not to mention the princess he was supposed to marry.

"Under the circumstances," he said, stepping into the stirrup, "I think we should part ways."

He swung his leg over the saddle and settled into position. She hurried to the side of his horse, looking up at him with those big, green imploring eyes.

The soldier had said he was looking for a girl with blonde hair and green eyes. He had no doubt in his mind Rose was the girl.

"Please wait," she implored.

He remained where he was, gazing down at her waiting for her to say something. She scanned the town and licked her lips, as though coming to a decision.

"If you'll ride out of town with me, then I'll tell you why the men were looking for me." Her gaze lifted back to his.

Her pleading gaze that begged him not to turn her over to the guards or separate from her. His resolve melted into a puddle. He pushed out a breath, his shoulders slumping a little.

"All right, then."

She hurried to her horse and climbed into the saddle. Moments later, they were off, trotting through town and heading for the gates.

Her mind raced as they rode along in silence. If she told him the truth about who she was, would he even believe her? She had to come up with something to tell him. Something that he *would* believe. But what?

They were almost out of the town gates. Her nerves were wound so tight, her stomach cramped and threatened to heave the delicious meal she'd just had. She swallowed hard, trying to keep her wits about her.

At the town gates, he halted and gave her a pointed look. "Well?"

There were still too many people within earshot for her comfort. She eyed the forest ahead.

"Let's ride into the forest." She glanced back to see if they were followed, but no one was there.

"And then you'll tell me?" he asked.

"Yes," she said with a nod.

They continued on. But as they approached the forest, she still had not come up with a plausible reason why the soldiers were looking for her. She decided to stick as close to the truth as possible.

Once they were through the trees and in the cover of the forest, she reined in her horse. He did the same, looking at her with an expectant expression as he leaned on the saddle horn.

"I ran away from home," she said at last.

A brow lifted in curiosity. "And home is?"

She swallowed hard, her mouth turning dry. "Myst Hall."

Edward's brows drew together in question. "And the soldiers want to take you back there, I gather."

"Yes," she said with a nod. She focused her gaze on the cluster of trees in front of her. The smell of bracken and damp leaves wafted to her nose. "I don't want to go back."

"Why not?" he asked.

Anything she answered would give her true persona away. She dragged her lower lip through her teeth and tried to come up with a plausible response.

"Are you the daughter of a noble?" he asked.

A laugh nearly bubbled up her throat, but she managed to contain it. She glanced at him. "You could say that."

He still leaned on the saddle horn. His handsome features were creased with perplexity. Golden strands of his hair shone in the afternoon light shafting through the trees. He tipped his head to the side and gave her a lopsided grin.

"Are you running away from an arranged marriage?" He said it as though it were a farce.

Her heart thudded. "Yes."

His cocky grin melted away replaced by something akin to empathy. "I understand that."

"You do?"

Rosamund met his gaze and her pulse skipped. His expression softened, as though he truly did understand. He straightened in the saddle, then shifted.

"More than you know," he muttered.

She took a deep breath and decided to throw away her caution. "The truth is I am betrothed to the prince of Woodhaven."

His head snapped to her, his eyes wide with surprise. "You..." The word came out a breath. He swallowed hard, regaining his composure. "But...to be betrothed to a prince, you'd have to be—"

"A princess. And I am." She refused to meet his gaze. "The Princess of Myst. Daughter of King Stephan and Queen Eleanor."

"The princess...of Myst Hall." He sounded incredulous, his voice a roughened whisper.

She glanced at him to gauge his reaction. His expression was unreadable, his eyes shadowed as though deep in thought.

"My parents didn't tell me I was betrothed until the day the king and queen of Woodhaven arrived. My wedding was already planned a few days after my birthday. That's why I ran away. I do not wish for my life to be controlled and planned for me." She clutched the reins tighter in her hands until they cramped.

"You are Princess Rosamund. Aren't you?" he asked.

The sound of her name rolling off his tongue sent a little thrill through her. Heat crawled up her neck and pierced her cheeks. "Yes. Are you going to hand me over to the soldiers?"

He considered this as he looked at her, then he shook his head slowly. "No, I am not."

"Because you could," she continued, as though trying to convince him. "And likely fetch a nice price for returning me to my father. He would pay handsomely for my safe return, no doubt."

There was a bitterness in her tone. A bitterness she hadn't expected to hear. Did she want to return? No, not ever. But if this man insisted on finding the soldiers and handing her over, she would have no choice but to go.

"I'm not going to turn you in," he said, his voice soft.

"You're not?"

"No," he said. "They're likely looking for you in the next town over." His dazzling smile was reassuring. "If we keep to the trees, they likely won't follow us."

"Do you think so?" Her voice was quiet, almost timid, and she hated herself for that.

"I do. And, I think we should continue our journey. That is, if you'd like to continue along with me."

Relief sputtered through her. "I would like that very much."

"Good. Then perhaps we'll find that adventure yet." He gave her a surreptitious wink as he took up the reins and nudged his horse into a walk.

She followed him, her heart pounding a wild beat as she thought of facing adventure with him. She hoped it was a grand one.

For a moment, Rowena thought the two were going to split in the town near Mystwood Forest. Relief spread through her like wildfire when she saw them continue to travel together.

Curses on those Myst Hall soldiers. They nearly ruined everything. She used a bit of her Fae magic to send them on a wild goose chase to keep them from finding the girl. She couldn't have that. Not yet.

The girl's birthday was in three days. By then, the two of them would be exactly where she wanted them. A broad smile crossed her face.

It was time for her to sift and greet them at last.

CHAPTER 14

Phillip could not believe it. Here he was journeying with the woman he was supposed to marry. He was to meet Princess Rosamund upon his arrival. Yet, he had run away for the same reasons. He didn't want his life controlled and planned for him by his parents or hers.

The fact she didn't want to marry him either was almost humorous. And for a moment, he was offended until he cast it aside and thought about what she'd told him. How awful she didn't know of their betrothal until a few days ago, for he knew when his parents left Haven Castle and when they arrived in Myst. He was supposed to be with them.

Perhaps they were not so unalike after all.

He almost wanted to laugh out loud at the coincidence that they felt the same way about each other. Was their meeting simply chance or something more? Kismet, perhaps?

He, of course, was aware of the betrothal from the time he was six years old. When he stood at the baby princess's christening and watched the Fae royals from the Fae Courts arrive and bestow their gifts upon her.

As he and Rosamund rode on deeper into the forest, he searched his memories for those Fae gifts. What was the first one the strange and elegant queen bestowed upon her? Ah, yes. Beauty, charm, and grace.

He glanced at her. Beauty. She certainly had that with hair reminiscent of spun gold. Her eyes were big and bright and the darkest green he had ever seen. Like emeralds. She had grown from the squalling baby he recalled into a beautiful young woman.

Charm and grace? At the cabin, she had gone out of her way to see to his comfort. As far as grace, she walked in a way with her shoulders squared, her head held high, her back straight. If he was paying attention, he'd realize she was more than a mere peasant girl. Even now as she rode in the saddle, she held her head high and kept her back straight.

Phillip tried to recall the other gifts of the Fae, but could not. Except for one in particular. One from a dark faery who was inadvertently left off the guest list for the festivities. She exacted her wrath on the baby girl.

The words leapt to his mind.

Before the sun sets on her eighteenth birthday, she will prick her finger on the thorn of a rose and die.

It was only due to the remaining Fae queen who had not yet presented her gift to the princess that she was able to change it from a death curse to a sleeping curse.

He looked her way once more, eyeing her as he remembered the horror that had rippled through the assembly. How her mother, Queen Eleanor, had wept with despair when she thought her daughter would die. How her father, King Stephan, ordered the removal of all roses from the castle grounds immediately.

She said the wedding—their wedding—was planned a few days after her birthday. Her *eighteenth* birthday. Judging by the fact she was still awake meant she had not yet pricked her finger on a thorn. Which also meant her birthday hadn't come to pass. Did she know she was cursed to fall into a forever slumber?

If she didn't know about their betrothal, it seemed reasonable to him she wouldn't know about the curse.

Rosamund must have sensed him looking at her for she turned her head and met his gaze. A hint of a smile played at the corners of her mouth.

"You're staring," she said.

He turned away. "Apologies. It's just that I was wondering if I should address you as your highness now."

"No," she snapped. "You will address me as Rosamund. The princess disappeared the moment I fled the castle."

Surprise flickered through him at her statement. She was determined, it seemed, to cast aside the princess and become someone else. Was the thought of marrying him so terrible?

They rode on in silence into the forest. He tried to coax more information out of her.

"You mentioned your birthday," he said. "Is it soon?"

Her eyes remained forward, pinned on the trees ahead. She stiffened. "Soon enough." She paused for a long moment, then said in a low voice, "My birthday doesn't matter."

Oh, but it did. If only she knew how much it mattered. Now that he knew her true identity, vigilance was his constant companion. He'd make sure she wouldn't prick her finger on any thorns and fall into a deep sleep.

"Well, it matters to me," he said, sounding cheerful. "When is it? We should celebrate."

She laughed. "I think not."

"Why not? Birthdays are important," he prodded, hoping to get her to tell him.

Rosamund huffed out a breath. "It's in three days."

Three days. He had three days to be on his guard and make sure she didn't go anywhere near roses with thorns.

"Well, then, in three days we'll celebrate."

She cast him an annoyed glance at his cheerful exuberance that made him stifle a chuckle.

As they rode farther into the forest, the day began to wane. He realized they would have to make camp for the night. He doubted she was accustomed to sleeping outside, but if she were to become an adventurer instead of a princess, then it was something she'd have to get used to.

They arrived in a small clearing with a felled tree. The log had moss growing on one side. Tall trees surrounded the small area, shrouding it in shadows. He halted a moment, his keen eyes taking in their surroundings. Then he gave a quick nod.

"I think we should camp here for the night," he said.

"Here?" Her frown of dismay was evident.

"Yes." He dismounted and tied up his horse. "I'll gather wood for a fire."

"Don't go too far," she said, sounding uneasy.

As he scanned the area for wood, she dismounted and tied up her horse next to his. He caught a glimpse of her patting the animal's neck with affection.

"Perhaps there is water nearby," she said to the mare, continuing to stroke her neck. "You deserve a big bag of oats for all of this, don't you?"

The mare replied with a snort, as though she understood.

When he had an armload of wood, he stepped back into the small clearing and began building the fire. She watched with great interest as he placed the wood into a pyramid. Then he tossed dried leaves around it and in between the logs. Returning to his saddle bags, he retrieved his matches and lit one of the leaves. It caught fire immediately and moments later they had a warm blaze.

He stepped back, grinning, clearly pleased with his handiwork.

"How do you know how to do that?" she asked.

"My father and I used to hunt when I was a child," he said. "He taught me."

Rosamund sat on the ground by the log, drawing up her knees. The firelight flickered over her features. She had a pensive look about her as she wrapped her arms around her legs and rested her chin on her knees.

"Is hunting fun?"

He returned once again to his saddlebags and drew out the wrapped food he had swiped from the castle kitchen before he left. It had only just occurred to him he still had the wheel of cheese and the loaf of bread. He sat down next to her and unwrapped the food.

"I suppose it is. When he was too busy to take me, I went with friends."

He thought of Charles and Jeffrey—the friends he hunted and hawked with. He wondered how furious Jeffrey was when he discovered he was gone from the keep without him.

Taking out his dagger, he sliced off pieces of cheese and then bread and handed them to her. She took them with a grateful smile.

"I suppose that means you won't be hunting us any dinner other than this." She lifted the piece of bread.

Phillip sliced more cheese for himself. "You don't like my cooking?" He couldn't resist the barb.

"I like your cooking fine," she replied. "Especially since it means we won't starve. I'm grateful for it, really."

"You're welcome."

A twig snapped. He sat up straighter, his hand still clutching the hilt of his dagger as he peered into the shadows. She heard it, too. Her head snapped in the direction of the noise. Even the horses seemed restless.

"What was that?" she whispered.

Another twig, which could only be that of another person. He handed her the dagger. She gave him a wide-eyed look of surprise.

"In case," he whispered.

He got to his feet, his hand on the hilt of his sword.

An old woman emerged from the shadows, her back hunched as she stumbled into their makeshift camp. She wore a black gown, tattered at the hem and the edges of her sleeves. The cloak she had over her shoulders didn't fare much better. Her nose was hooked and large. Her face a map of wrinkles. Her black hair was tied back away from her face at the nape of her neck, but sprigs of wiry hair sprung out from her head in all directions.

She paused by a tree, her gnarled hand on the bark to steady herself as she peered at them with squinting eyes.

"Ah, so ye're the source of the fire in me forest," the hag said in a roughened voice.

He relaxed his stance but kept his hand on the hilt. Next to him, Rosamund gripped the dagger. The old woman's beady gaze landed on it. She cackled.

"Ye can put that away now, dearie. I mean no harm."

"Are you lost?" he asked.

"Lost?" She cackled again. "Nay, my good man. You two appear to be needing shelter for the night. My cabin is just there." She pointed a gnarled finger over her shoulder in a direction behind her.

Phillip extended his hand to Rosamund for the dagger. Reluctantly, she handed it over and he sheathed it. Peering at the old woman, he wasn't sure he trusted her. And why should he? It seemed odd the old woman appeared out the shadows with an offer of shelter for the night.

A glance at Rosamund told him she had the same thought.

"I have a nice warm fire and a couple of cozy beds for ye both," she said. "I can even feed ye a better meal than that. Bring yer horses. I can feed and water them, too."

Rosamund met his level gaze. Question burned deep within those emerald eyes of hers.

"I see yer hesitation," the woman said. "I mean ye no harm. Truly. I'll give ye a moment to discuss."

She melted into the shadows, disappearing as quickly as she had appeared. Phillip moved closer to her, his sleeve brushing hers.

"What do you think?" he asked, his voice low. "Can we trust her?"

She shook her head. "I don't think so, but for the chance at a nice bed and a warm meal..." Her words trailed off.

"Indeed," he agreed. "All right, then. We follow her. I'll stay on my guard and we can leave at first light."

She nodded agreement. He kicked dirt on the fire, snuffing it out. It plunged them in total darkness. She drew in a sudden, sharp breath. Another cackle from the old hag and suddenly a ball of blue-white light appeared between two trees.

"Come along, dearies."

He untied the horses, handing her the reins of her mare. As he passed, he was aware of the skeptical look on her face. Even so, she fell in step beside him and, together, they followed the old woman through the trees to her cabin in the woods.

Chapter 15

T he cabin was large with yellow light glowing in the windows and a chimney that had gray smoke curling upward into the night sky. As they approached, apprehension swept through Rosamund. Her gut clenched. There was no explanation for that reaction since the old woman seemed to want to help.

She looked at Edward to gauge his reaction, but it was difficult to see his expression in the shadows. She shoved away those irrational feelings and decided to accept the help from the old woman for what it was—a kind offer.

At the cabin, the woman shoved open the door. Light slashed from the doorway, outlining her hunched silhouette.

"Ye can leave yer horses here." She pointed to the left of the door. Then she waved them inside. "Come in, come in. Warm yeselves by the fire."

She bustled inside and waited for them to enter before closing the door with a snap behind them. Inside, a fire blazed in the hearth, warming the room and chasing the chill from Rosamund's bones. The furniture was well-worn but looked comfortable. Two chairs were on either side of the fireplace. A near threadbare rug was on the wood slated floor. Toward the back of the cabin was a loft with a narrow, winding staircase leading upward.

In the kitchen, a scarred wooden table with four chairs. The old woman bustled about, humming a low tune to herself as she prepared the meal she promised.

Edward moved toward the fireplace, extending his hands to warm them. But Rosamund remained in place as she watched the woman in the kitchen. That eerie sensation something was amiss did not want to leave her.

The old woman placed two bowls on the table, then returned to the kitchen and brought a small platter with fresh baked bread. Seeing that made Rosamund's stomach rumble with such force, she was almost faint.

"As promised." She waved to the table. "Food for ye."

Rosamund glanced at Edward. Their eyes met for a brief moment before he moved toward the table and took a seat in front of one of the bowls. She followed his lead and sat next to him, gazing down at the bowl of what appeared to be potato and leek soup. He took up his spoon and dug in with enthusiasm.

"Do ye not like it, m'dear?" the old woman asked when she noticed she wasn't eating.

"Oh."

The word came out in a roughened whisper. She grabbed her spoon and stuck it in the bowl, aware of the woman's watchful gaze. She took a taste.

"It's delicious," she said. "Thank you."

"Good, good!" Then she was back in the small kitchen. She put a pot on to boil. "'Tis much better than sleeping in the woods, aye?"

"Your hospitality is quite generous," Edward said around a mouthful. He reached for the bread and tore a piece off, then dunked it in the soup.

"Och, it's the least I can do for two travelers who seemed to be lost and weary." She paused what she was doing to turn around and look at them both, her eyes narrowed in a sharp squint. "Ye are lost, aren't ye? No one ventures into these woods with purpose."

They both stared at her in stunned silence. Finally, Edward replied.

"We're not lost. Merely passing through."

The kettle whistled then. She pulled it off the stove and poured the steaming water into two mugs, then brought them over to the table and dropped them down in front of them. The strong scent of bergamot wafted to her nose. Rosamond was so happy to have a cup of freshly brewed tea, she dropped her spoon and immediately reached for her cup. She held the mug under her nose, inhaling the scent as her eyes fluttered closed.

"Oh, my favorite," she breathed.

The woman cackled with delight. "Good to hear it, dear." Then to Edward, she said, "Passing through, eh? Where ye headed?"

Rosamund gave him a sideways glance. He seemed unflustered by the questions. "Wherever the wind takes us."

She almost laughed at his reply and the subsequent crooked grin he flashed her.

"Ah, so ye are a bit of an adventurer, then."

The woman brought her own bowl and mug to the table and took a spot across from him. The steam rose from her mug, curling upward in a bit of a white cloud.

"What are ye names?" she asked.

"I'm Edward," he answered, before she could. "This is Rose. And you are?"

"Olga," the woman said. Her eyes drifted from Edward back to her, narrowing a bit. "Rose, ye say?"

"Yes," she replied on a breath, then took a sip of tea. "Your hospitality is quite generous, Olga."

"'Tis nothing." She dunked her spoon into the soup and slurped. "If yer looking for a bit of adventure, I hear there's a dragon deep within a cave of these woods that guards a glittering treasure of immense wealth." As Olga said this, broth dribbled down her chin.

"Treasure?" Edward sat straighter in his chair, his meal forgotten. "What sort of treasure?"

"Gold, jewels and the like," the old woman said with a wave of her hand.

"I thought dragons were nothing more than myths," Rosamund said.

"Not a myth, dearie," Olga said. "I've seen the dragon meself."

"Have you?" Edward sounded intrigued. He learned forward. "You know the treasure exists?"

"O'course, I do. I seen it with me own eyes." She flashed a toothy grin, showing off stump teeth. Then dug back into the soup.

Edward sat back in the chair. His gaze drifted from the old woman to Rosamund. Deep in the honey color depths, she saw the glint of excitement. In fact, she felt that zing of excitement from him, almost as though she read his mind.

She shook her head to indicate she was not interested in chasing dragons or looking for treasure. He lifted one brow as if to reply she was missing out on the adventure for which she longed. Then she tipped her head to one side in a silent reply to tell him he was out of his mind.

"I see I've caught yer attention. I have a map to the cave. That is, if ye have an interest."

Olga had witnessed the silent exchange and was clearly intent on encouraging the quest.

"I'm interested," he said. "I'd like to see the map."

Rosamund dropped her hand into her lap, clenching her fist. The thought of heading deeper into the forest looking for a dragon who likely protected its treasures with deadly force did not sound like a good idea to her.

Olga, however, grinned with triumph as she pushed her old body from the table and shuffled off to another room. Rosamund leaned toward him and dropped her voice to whisper.

"Do you think this wise?" she asked.

"Come now, princess. You said yourself you'd love a good adventure. I can't think of a better one than to hunt a dragon and see if this treasure really does exist." He flashed her a wicked grin.

Irritation simmered under the surface as she sat back in the chair, annoyed he flung her words back at her. She'd said that in a moment of dreamy hope, when she was still trying to figure out where she was going and what she was to do with the rest of her life. She had never expected to meet anyone to journey with, especially someone like Edward.

Though, she was starting to wonder who he truly was. Something told her he was hiding something, too. That perhaps he hadn't been completely honest with her, either.

Telling the truth about who she was felt as though a load was lifted from her shoulders. She was grateful he didn't want to hand her over to the soldiers. She paid close attention to his mannerisms and the way he spoke. He was definitely part of the nobility. Perhaps he was a lord from Woodhaven. But if he were, it did not explain why he traveled alone. A man of stature would have attendants. He did not.

And he had this insatiable need to chase the wind.

Was she so different?

As she pondered this, Olga shuffled back into the room with a rolled parchment clutched in one hand. She handed it over to Edward. He took it and shoved his bowl out of the way to unfurl it on the table in front of him. Rosamund stretched taller in her chair to get a good look at it.

Indeed, it was a map of Mystwood Forest with a trail leading right to a cave. He stared down at it, tracing his finger along the dotted line leading to the cave.

"In case yer wondering, yer not far from there." Olga picked up his discarded bowl with an encouraging smile and headed back into the small kitchen.

"How far away?" he asked.

"I'd say you'd be there in…" She paused, tapping a gnarled finger against her jutting chin and hmmed as she made the calculation in her mind. "…a couple of days."

"A couple of days," Rosamund repeated.

She and Edward exchanged a glance and she wondered if he was thinking what she was thinking. Her birthday was in a couple of days. A wide grin spread upon his face.

"Perfect," he said.

His eyes sparked with newfound resolve. Rosamund knew they were headed there in the morning.

"Mercy. Listen to me goin' on. I better see to yer horses."

Olga shuffled out of the cabin, leaving them alone. Rosamund sat back in her chair, her nerves jangling.

"I think we should do it," he said.

"Raid a dragon's cave for treasure?" She shook her head. "I think not."

But he was not to be dissuaded. "Think of it. We can split the treasure between us. And I can't think of a more perfect birthday present than that."

Fear clenched her gut. "I can think of a better one."

"What's that?"

"Not getting dead," she said. "Don't you think this dragon will be guarding it's treasure?"

"Of course," he replied, nonchalantly. "That's what makes it a grand adventure."

"You're crazy."

Still peering down at the map, he answered, "I've been told."

She pushed back from the table and rose, though she hadn't any idea where to go. Realizing that, she sat once again and huffed out a breath. He lifted his head, finally, and met her gaze. His shoulders slumped as his determination melted away.

"Do you not wish to go then?" he asked.

She fiddled with the spoon she'd placed on the table by her bowl, her soup forgotten. Apprehension swept through her. It was the same feeling she had when she decided to run away from the castle. Yet she'd done it anyway. She pushed aside the fear and took the risk and made it away from the keep without anyone noticing.

Wasn't this much the same thing? She was taking another risk. If she agreed, then it would be one more step further away from her old life. One more step away from being the princess she'd always been.

"I have a suggestion," he said, his voice soft. "Sleep on it."

Her gaze drifted back to his. "Sleep on it?"

"Yes. When I have a difficult decision to make, I like to sleep on it and decide in the morning." He rolled up the map and sat back in the chair. "What do you say?"

Slowly, she nodded. "All right."

Just as she said it, Olga bustled back inside. "Horses are fed. Och, ye must be tired from yer travels. Come on, then. I'll show ye to yer room."

"Room?" Rosamund asked.

She gave a toothy grin. "'Fraid I only have one." She waved for them to follow.

Edward clutched the rolled-up map in his hand. They both got to their feet as she led them to the winding staircase at the back of the cabin.

"Up here," she said, pointing. "Two beds. One fer each of ye. Be gone before daylight."

"Why?" Rose asked, suspicious.

"Why, to find the treasure, o'course. Good night!"

Then she was off, disappearing into one of the other rooms of the cabin and closing the door with a snap.

They stood there, each of them in stunned silence, until at last he motioned for her to take the first step.

"After you, my lady," he said.

She started up the stairs, trepidation following her.

CHAPTER 16

U p the winding wood staircase she went and stepped into the loft that was shrouded in darkness. Edward followed and halted next to her. He fumbled in his pocket and a moment later, she heard him strike a match.

True to her word, there were two narrow beds with a table between them. On the table, an oil lamp. He went to it and lit it. The yellow light illuminated the small loft in a soft glow.

"Well, it's not much, but she did say she had beds for us," he said.

He removed his sword belt and dagger and placed it on the floor by the bed, then perched on the one closest to the staircase. She took the one near the wall with the one window covered by shear curtains. She pushed back the material and peered out through the window but saw nothing but darkness and trees.

With a sigh, she sat on the bed and pulled off her boots, dropping them on the floor with a thunk.

"I suppose it will do," she said.

She swung her feet up on the bed and laid back, rolling to her side to face him. She curled her arm under the pillow, her eyes heavy. He was seated in the center of his bed, his long legs stretched out and the map on his lap as he studied it some more.

Something he said came back to her. That they could split the treasure between them. He was already dreaming of treasures and gold and they hadn't even left yet. And what if they did find the treasure? Then what? They split it between them and go their separate ways? Though he hadn't said it, she sensed that's what he inferred. She stifled a yawn, watching him as he muttered to himself about routes and how to get to the cave. There was a definite excitement emanating off him.

"Perhaps the old woman would give us some provisions before we go," he said, more to himself than her. "We'd need a couple of water flasks. Then we could ride straight through to the dragon's lair."

Something about all of this didn't sit right with her. From the moment Olga made an appearance in the woods and found them, she had the distinct feeling something was amiss. It was difficult to ignore her roiling stomach.

"Don't you think it's odd she *happened* to come upon us? And that her cabin *happened* to be nearby?" Rosamund asked.

He lifted his head from the map to look at her. "Do *you* think it's odd?"

Another yawn threatened but she pushed it away. "It seems rather coincidental she found us. And why tell us about the treasure? Why doesn't she go after it herself?"

"Have you *seen* the woman?" he asked, his voice laced with sarcasm.

But Rosamund ignored him and went on. She flopped to her back and stared at the ceiling. "And the map. It was quite handy she had the map ready to give you after she interested you with talk of gold and jewels."

"You think I'm only interested in gold and jewels?" He sounded wounded.

She glanced over at him. "You're not?"

He turned away, leaning his head back on the fluffy pillows and blowing out a breath. "When I was younger, I wanted nothing more than to be a hunter. But my father..." He paused, his mind working as he chose his next words. "My father didn't want that for me."

"You said you hunted with friends," she reminded him. "Oh, wait. That's wrong. You said you liked to sit in taverns with your friends and drink ale."

His lips thinned into a straight line. "How well you remember, princess. What I'm trying to say is this would be an opportunity to finally..."

"Be the hunter you always wanted to be?" she asked.

"Something like that."

She understood what he was doing. He was trying to convince her. Still, she had reservations about the whole thing and she couldn't help but feel as though the ordeal was contrived by Olga.

There was something strangely familiar about her. Something that set off her senses that told her not to trust her. Yet Edward was ready to throw caution to the wind.

She peered at the map resting on his lap and wondered if it would be the grand adventure she dreamed of. Her heart skipped a little at the thought. The impulse to go was pounding through her but she said she would sleep on it. And truthfully, her eyelids were heavy and all she really wanted to do was sleep.

He gave her a weak smile. "I suppose we can decide in the morning."

"I suppose we can," she muttered, her voice thick with fatigue. "Good night, Edward."

"Good night, Rose."

During the night, Rosamund awoke. For a moment, she didn't recall where she was and it took several seconds to reorient herself to her surroundings. She glanced at the window, darkened by the nighttime shadows. Everything came back to her in a rush. Her pulse raced as she thought of going on a grand adventure to search for a dragon's treasure.

It was likely a foolhardy quest, not to mention dangerous. What if the dragon was there guarding its treasure?

And if it wasn't, and they found it...

She would have the means to truly start a new life somewhere else.

Her parents would be brokenhearted. Guilt swept through her. Could she truly take a step into a life of independence? A life that did not include servants and luxury? A life that did not include a loveless marriage?

Rosamund sat up in the bed, her heart racing. She watched the sleeping form in the bed next to hers, his chest rising and falling in rhythmic breathing patterns indicating he was fast asleep. She had to tell him now, though, before she lost her nerve.

Slipping from the bed, she gave him a gentle shake. "Edward?"

He grunted in response but didn't wake.

"Wake up," she said with another shake.

His eyes popped open as he lunged from the bed, reaching for her. She stumbled back, her hands outstretched.

"It's me! Rosamund!"

He huffed out a breath. "Gods, you scared me."

"I'm sorry. I just wanted to tell you..." She paused as her breath hitched.

"Tell me what?" He rubbed his eyes.

"Let's do it. Let's find the treasure."

"That? That's what you wanted to tell me?" He frowned at her.

"Yes."

"You could have waited until morning," he grumbled.

"No, I couldn't wait," she said. "I had to tell you now. Good night."

With that, she crawled back into her bed and pulled up the bedcovers. Before too long she was fast asleep.

CHAPTER 17

"R ose, wake up."

It was Edward's urgent voice in her ear as he shook her. She blinked open her eyes to see him standing in between the two beds with the strangest look of confusion mixed with unease on his face. She was instantly wide awake and on high alert.

"We have to go." There was an urgency in his voice that alarmed her.

"What is it? What's wrong?"

The moment she sat up in the bed, she knew. The cabin they were in had somehow changed overnight. She glanced at the window where there had once been shear curtains. Those were gone. The glass was grimy, making it difficult to see outside. Overhead, the roof of the cabin had holes in it, letting in slashes of morning light.

Odd. That wasn't there last night.

"Come *on*," he said even more urgent.

She sprang from the bed and reached for her boots. He was already moving to the staircase as she pulled them on. She grabbed her cloak from the end of the bed and followed. Once she was at the stairs, though, she halted in confusion. The staircase was not winding as before. Instead, it was replaced by rickety steps that went straight down.

"I don't understand," she said, clutching the handrail.

"You said that old hag finding us was a coincidence. I think you may have been right." He paused at the bottom of the stairs and glanced back up at her. "Let's go."

She took the stairs as quickly as she dared. Each one creaked and each one wobbled under her feet. By the time she was at the bottom, he was already out the door but she had paused to take another look around.

The table they sat at the previous night was covered in dust and dirt. The chairs were rickety. The fireplace that had a bright cheerful fire was now dark and cold. The kitchen was in shambles.

"What is going on?"

"Rose!" he shouted from the door.

When she snapped her head in his direction, he waved her out of the cabin. She hurried outside after him. He stood by the horses, holding the reins. When she turned to get a look at the cabin, she saw it was nothing more than a ramshackle building.

"She said be gone before daylight," she said, gaping at the place.

"Right," he agreed and pushed her reins into her hands. "We need to go."

He was in the saddle and riding off before she managed a foot in the stirrup. Hurrying to catch up, she quickly mounted the horse and turned to follow him.

"You were right, Rose," he said as the trotted away from the cabin.

"Right about what?"

He jerked his head back toward the cabin but said nothing.

"It was a spell, wasn't it?" She didn't know why she whispered it, but it seemed like the thing to do. As though the forest might have ears. "Was she a witch, you think?"

He flattened his lips as skepticism flickered over his face. "I don't believe in witches." He paused, then glanced her way. "But I do believe in faeries."

"Faeries?" she repeated and almost laughed.

"Yes," he said, emphatic. "Dark and evil ones."

Her brows drew together. "You think Olga was an evil faery?"

"What else would she be?" he asked.

He sounded so convincing, she wanted to believe him. "I don't know."

Silence stretched between them until he finally said, "Have you never heard of one?"

"No," she replied. "Have you?"

"Yes. I heard a story once about an evil faery who cursed a baby girl." He gave her a surreptitious glance.

"Why would a faery do such a thing?" she demanded, clutching the reins in her hand until her fingers cramped.

"Because she was angry she wasn't invited to—" he paused, pressing his lips together again and then finished with, "—a party."

"Sounds petty," she said. "What sort of curse?"

"A death curse," he said. "That if the baby girl pricked her finger on a thorn, she would die."

As he said it, a strange sensation came over her, almost as though she had heard this story before. But she hadn't. Her skin prickled with gooseflesh as the strange sensation went over her.

"How awful," she muttered.

"No one has ever told you that story?" he wanted to know.

She shook her head. "Did the baby die?"

"No," he said. "Another faery came along and changed the curse. Instead of dying when she pricked her finger, the girl would fall into an eternal slumber."

"Well, that's not much better, is it?" Rosamund said. "How is the curse broken?"

"I don't know."

He had a strange look on his face. One she was unable to read. As though he were telling this story for a reason, yet had not revealed that reason.

"So, you think this...evil faery created the cabin for us and lured us there. For what reason?"

"To give us the map to the dragon's treasure," he said, as if he were speaking of nothing serious.

"And put us in the path of peril on purpose? Again, I ask for what reason?"

Rosamund considered this as they continued to ride through the trees down a well-worn path. She had thought it was strange the night before. There was something that didn't sit right with the entire encounter with the old woman. Something that made her senses tingle.

"I have no answer to that, but I think you were right to question it," he added. "You're also right not to go after the treasure."

Disappointment flooded her. It had taken a great bit of courage for her to admit she wanted to go after the treasure. The grand adventure was slipping away from her.

"You said you wanted to be a hunter," she reminded him.

He nodded. "I did. I do."

"And now you think we should forget about it?"

"Perhaps we should," he said.

She bit her bottom lip to keep from crying out with her objections. Last night, when she was sitting at the table with the bowl of soup, she felt there was something awry about the whole situation. But there was such a light of excitement in his eyes. It left her wondering what she was going to do to live out her days as a peasant since she wasn't planning on returning to her life as a princess.

"Where are we headed?" she asked, abruptly changing the subject.

"Northwest. I thought once we were out of the Mystwood Forest, we'd continue onward to Rothbridge. There are a few towns in between here and there where we can find food and rest."

If she recalled her geography correctly, Rothbridge was a kingdom northwest of Stonebridge.

"All right," she replied.

And though she didn't say it, she decided she would find a way to stay behind in one of those towns and start her new life.

It was near midday. Their conversation had gone to almost nothing except for a few comments here and there. She noticed he had stuck the rolled-up map in one of his saddle bags. It was slightly smashed, the end peeking out.

Rosamund found she could not stop thinking about the dragon's treasure. Perhaps there was a way for her to take the map and, once they split up, double back to find it herself. She hadn't totally given up the idea.

Likely she was crazy to even think about it, but since she'd made up her mind to go, she couldn't let it go.

"Ho there!" A voice called out.

They both twisted in the saddle to see two riders trotting toward them. It was two men. One waved in greeting, a big smile on his face.

"Bollocks," he said under his breath and came to a halt.

She, too, halted her horse and watched as the men came forward. One was strikingly handsome with blond hair and bright blue eyes that twinkled with mirth. The other man, who looked quite similar to the first, had a serious expression on his face.

"You're quite cunning, my prince," the man with the serious expression said. "We thought we'd never catch up to you."

"Prince?" She snapped her head in his direction, peering at him as question flooded her. "You're a prince?"

"Rose—" he began.

But the man cut him off. "He is, my lady. How fortune for you to be traveling with him. I'm glad to see his reputation as a rogue continues."

Rosamund sat rigid in the saddle as she gaped at him. Color rose high in his cheeks. He narrowed his gaze at the man, his brows drawing together in consternation.

"What are you doing here, Jeffrey?" he demanded.

"I'm here to do what I promised your mother I'd do. Take to you Myst Hall," Jeffrey said.

A gasp exploded from her. "Myst Hall?"

A flush crept up Edward's face as he gave her an apologetic glance. Then her eyes widened as understanding dawned. She was right to believe he was more than a peasant. She suspected a noble of some sort but she did not suspect he was Prince Phillip, her betrothed. Fury erupted through her. Fury along with a healthy dose of embarrassment.

"Prince Phillip, is it?" she asked, her tone laced with acid. "You lied to me."

"With all due respect, princess, you lied to me, too," he countered.

"Princess?" The one with the bright blue eyes peered at her as shock registered on his face. "This is Princess Rosamund?"

"I told you the truth," she snapped, ignoring the outburst. "You could have done the same when you knew who I was. Yet you didn't. You let me believe you were nothing more than a...a...peasant!"

Jeffrey chortled. But Phillip found her intended remark to be an insult. Good. She meant for it to be.

"Rose—" Phillip said.

"Do *not* call me that."

She clutched the reins in her hands and did the only thing she could think of to do. She kicked her horse into action and fled.

Chapter 18

Rosamund's mount galloped between Phillip and the other men. She heard him calling for her to wait, to stop. But she didn't want to stop. Her heart was pounding a wicked beat. The flames of fury burned within her, threatening to consume all that she was.

To think, she thought him handsome! That she liked him. That she went out of her way to bring him cushions and blankets when they spent the night in the first cabin. What a fool she'd been.

She'd told him things. That she didn't want to be married to someone she had never met. That he was *that* person. Hot tears of anger at his deception burned through her.

Ahead, she saw a clearing and headed for it. Behind her, she heard the pounding of another horse and knew he followed. She urged her horse onward, faster. So fast, she saw the limb hanging down too late to avoid it. She ducked, but the end of it scraped across her cheek. A stinging sensation erupted in the cool breeze. She felt the dampness of blood.

"Rose, wait!" he called after her.

She threw a look over her shoulder to see he was nearly upon her. He was a better rider than she was, she had to admit, and was closing the gap. The other two men were right behind him as they chased her down.

"Yah!" she shouted, urging her horse to go faster.

It was not enough. He caught up to her, pulling alongside her as they entered the clearing. He was close. So close he reached for her reins. She batted his hand away.

"Go away!" she shouted.

"Rose, please. Let me explain."

Her mount stumbled in a divot in the ground and came to an abrupt screeching halt. She was thrown from the saddle and landed with a thud in a thick tuft of grass that managed to cushion most of her fall. She managed to roll out of the way before she was trampled by her spooked horse. She was on her back, staring up at the late afternoon sky with wispy clouds. A quick inventory and she realized everything hurt from head to toe. The next thing she saw was Phillip's face in her line of vision. Concern etched his features as he slipped an arm around her. He pulled her into his lap and cradled her to his chest.

"Are you all right?"

She glared up at him, the fire still burning through her. She pressed her lips together, wishing she had the energy to shove him away. As it was, she was rather weak and in a lot of pain.

"Your cheek is bleeding but it looks like only a scratch. Is anything broken?" His hand slipped down one arm, feeling the bone.

Again, she wanted to bat his hand away but it hurt too much to move. Still, she didn't think she had broken anything.

"I'm fine," she muttered.

"That was quite a tumble she took." She recognized Jeffrey's voice. He had dismounted and moved to stand in front of them. "Is the princess all right?"

"The *princess* is quite awake and aware you're talking about her as if she were unconscious," Rosamund spat.

"Quite the spitfire, isn't she?" the other man said.

Jeffrey gave him a half-hearted shove with his elbow. "Quiet, Charles."

"Both of you shush," Phillip snapped. Then he turned his attention back to her, his expression softening. "Rose?"

"I told you not to call me that."

She pushed away from him, sliding out of his lap and into the cool grass. She swiped her hand over her stinging cheek. The scratch must have been shallow for there was no more blood. She glanced down to see a grass stain on one elbow. Likely where she landed and skidded to halt her fall. The knees of her pants also had dark green grass stains. Meanwhile, her horse was happily grazing on the other side of the clearing.

"Let me help you up." He wrapped a hand around her upper arm.

"I don't your help, *prince*."

She shoved him off and struggled to her feet. She wobbled a moment and realized one ankle throbbed with a sharp, burning pain. When she tried to take a step, she lost her balance. But Phillip was there to catch her and keep her from tumbling to the ground again.

"Unhand me," she snapped.

"It's your ankle, isn't it?" Jeffrey asked. "Best get that boot off before it swells."

"Jeffrey, where's the nearest town or village?" Phillip asked.

"More than a day's ride," he said. "We won't make it before nightfall."

He wrapped an arm around her waist to keep her upright. As much as she wanted to shrug him off, she knew if she did, she would regret it. For now, she was able to put most of her weight on her good leg and lean into him.

Phillip glanced around the clearing. "We best make camp here tonight."

"Here?" She balked at the idea of being in the open at night.

Though she was willing the night before, she wasn't so fond of the idea now. Her ankle hurt, her elbow throbbed, and she was angry with Phillip for his continued deception. She wished they were at an inn and she had a room to herself so she could think.

"I don't see any inns with featherbeds, your highness, so yes, here," Jeffrey chided.

She shot him a glare as she frowned.

"That will be quite enough, Jeffrey," Phillip said. "Make camp, will you? I'll see to the princess."

She hissed out a breath. "You'll do no such thing."

"Jeffrey is right. You need to get that boot off before your ankle swells and you can't get it off. Come on. I'll help you." He walked her toward the clearing where there was a fallen log.

Despite her anger with him, she was grateful for the help. She doubted she was able to walk across the clearing of her own volition. Her ankle *did* throb quite a bit.

"I don't like you very much right now," she muttered.

"I know."

"I'm angry with you," she said.

"I know that, too," he replied. "And you have every right to be. You're right. I should have told you straightaway who I was."

At the log, he helped her lower to the ground. She whimpered as her ankle twinged. She stretched out her legs as she leaned against the roughened bark. He knelt at her feet and reached for her left boot, then paused. He looked up at her, his brows raised in question.

"May I?" he asked.

She huffed out a breath. "Despite my better judgment, yes."

Phillip chuckled as he grasped her heel and gave a tug. She gasped as the pain lanced through her. She clenched her jaw tight to keep from crying out.

"I'm sorry," he said. "Try to relax."

"I'll try," she said through gritted teeth.

He tugged once more, and once more, she involuntarily gasped and fought back tears, the agony threatening to overwhelm her. When the boot slipped off her foot, she blew out the breath. He placed it aside and then began to examine her. His deft fingers moved along her foot and around her ankle, probing with a gentle touch. When he got to the soft place below her anklebone, she winced.

"That hurts?" he asked.

"Yes," she said on a breath.

He continued his probing. He grasped her stockinged foot in one hand and then gently flexed her foot.

"Does that hurt?" he asked.

"No."

Satisfied, he released her and sat back on his heels. "It doesn't appear to be broken. That's good news. I think you merely twisted it."

Behind him, Charles said something to Jeffrey who was busy rolling out a bedroll he'd pulled from the saddle bags. Charles had an armload of wood and dropped it on the ground, then built a small pyramid for a fire.

"So, who's Edward?" she asked, thinking of the alias he gave her.

"Edward is my grandfather's name."

She kept her gaze fixed on the two men working together.

"Are these your hunting friends?" she asked, watching as they built a small campsite.

Phillip glanced back at the two of them. "You might say that. I grew up with Jeffrey. Charles is his younger brother."

"And it's true Jeffrey was to bring you to Myst Hall?"

He met her gaze and gave a nod. "Yes. I managed to slip away for a 'hunting expedition,'" he put *hunting expedition* in air quotes, "when my parents were leaving to make the trek to your kingdom. I thought I could avoid my duties if I were not there to accompany them."

He moved to sit next to her, stretching out his long legs and crossing them at the ankles. He reached for a long stick with several green leaves on the end and picked them off one by one.

"You didn't want to go," she said, though it wasn't a question.

"No," he admitted.

"And you ran away," she said. "Like I did. Because you, like me, did not want to get married."

His gaze met hers. That feeling she had when they first met resurfaced, making her gut clench with a feeling she had not had before until she met Phillip. She didn't want to admit how handsome he was or even how comfortable she was when she was with him. He made her feel safe, even when they were in Olga's strange magical cabin that was clearly an illusion.

"Once again, your highness, it appears we are not so unalike."

"It would seem so."

She looked away, her hands clasped in her lap to keep from fidgeting. Her palms had broken into a hot sweat and yet still felt clammy. They watched Jeffrey and Charles continue to build the campsite. Charles started the fire, the flames tiny at first. He blew a breath to stoke the fire and moments later, it caught.

"So, I suppose we are to return to Myst Hall, then," she said, her voice flat.

Her heart thrummed at the thought of returning home with the prince, the very man she was supposed to marry. How would her parents react? Overjoyed she had managed to return with Phillip? Her birthday was day after tomorrow and then, a few days after that, the wedding.

Phillip picked a leaf off the branch, then tore it into tiny pieces. The pieces fluttered from his fingers into his lap. He brushed them away, then pulled off another leaf and repeated. His gaze was distant. Though he saw Charles and Jeffrey, he really did not *see* them.

"I suppose we are," he said at last, his voice as flat as hers.

He sounded as disappointed as she felt. Clearly, he did not want to marry her either. She couldn't decide if she should be insulted or not.

The thought of returning to her boring royal life did not bring her joy. The idea of an adventure hunting for dragon's treasure was now nothing more than a dream and a wish.

A shout rose up from Charles. He was on the other side of Phillip's horse and then emerged with the smashed rolled-up map in his hand, a broad smile on his face. Phillip growled, a sound low and deep in his throat. He shot to his feet and hurried toward Charles as he was unrolling the map.

"Well, what have we here?" Charles said it more to himself than anyone else as he crouched on the ground to examine the map.

"Put that back," Phillip shouted. He snatched the map from Charles and began to roll it up again. "That's not your concern."

"That was a map to a treasure," Charles said, rising to his feet and looking Phillip in the eye. "A map you weren't going to share with us."

Phillip glanced at Rosamund, who merely shrugged as if to say she had no opinion. The direction of their lives had changed and there was nothing either of them could do to stop it. Phillip looked back at Charles, clutching the map. Jeffrey joined them, peering at the roll.

"A treasure map, you say?" Jeffrey said.

"It's nothing," Phillip said.

She watched as he made to toss it into the fire and for some reason, a strangled cry escaped her.

"No, don't!" she shouted.

Phillip halted, clutching the map in his hand. His surprise was evident on his face as he looked at her. "Don't?" he asked.

"No," she said on a breath. "Tell them, Phillip."

Phillip looked back at the two men as he contemplated his words. "Gentlemen, this is a map to a treasure guarded by a dragon."

They both stared at him for a long moment, exchanged a glance and then burst out laughing.

Jeffrey said, "There are no dragons around here, Phillip."

In the distance, there was a faint sound. A *whump, whump* of what seemed like large wings. They all cast their gazes upward as the shadow blotted out the late afternoon sun. An outline of a dragon glided through the air.

Rosamund's eyes widened as she watched it traverse the sky.

"Are you sure about that, mate?" Phillip asked, humor in his voice.

Jeffrey leveled his gaze at his friend. "Perhaps you should show us that map."

CHAPTER 19

By nightfall, Phillip had helped Rosamund hobble from the fallen log so she could be closer to the fire. The cool night air was beginning to set in and chill her. Charles produced an extra bedroll from his saddle bag and laid it out for her. Jeffrey had a feast of bread, cheese, dried fruit, and oatcakes which he shared with all of them. Despite their initial unfortunate meeting, she was beginning to like the two men.

Phillip, Jeffrey, and Charles were at ease with each other. It was apparent to her Phillip was lifelong friends with Jeffrey. There was a sense of familiarity and comradery between them. Charles continued to sneak glances at her and then quickly look away when she noticed. And she noticed a lot.

It was endearing.

He was young with a shy smile and attentive to her needs. Since she was virtually immobile due to her sore ankle, he made sure she had enough to eat. He even had a flask of water which he shared with her. When she shivered from a cool breeze, he made sure she had her cloak.

Meanwhile, Phillip told them both of meeting the old woman in the strange cabin and how it morphed into a dilapidated building when they awoke the next morning.

He and Jeffrey were interested in the map and examined it closely, with Jeffrey scrutinizing it as though it were the most important document in the history of documents.

"I didn't know this cave existed," Jeffrey said, tapping the map with his forefinger.

"Nor did I," Phillip agreed, munching on an oatcake. "And yet we saw with our own eyes the dragon flying overhead."

"Do you think the treasure is really there?" Charles broke a piece of bread in half and popped a bit in his mouth.

"The old woman said it was," Phillip replied.

"But can we trust her after what we saw at the cabin?" Rosamund asked.

"She has a point," Jeffrey said. "Especially since the cabin you stayed in was clearly an illusion."

"Well, there's only one way to find out." Phillip glanced at her, a mischievous gleam in his eyes.

She recognized it immediately. "You think we should go after it, don't you?"

"Why not?" Phillip said.

"Because it's madness," Jeffrey pointed out. "And could be nothing but a wild goose chase."

Charles, who was silent for most of the conversation, finally said, "Why would the old woman want you two at the dragon's cave, though?"

Silence descended on their small camp. Rosamund glanced from Charles to Phillip who pressed his lips together as he considered the question.

"Why, indeed, is a good question, brother," Jeffrey said. He looked to Phillip. "What is this old woman's interest in the two of you?"

Phillip shrugged. "I haven't any idea."

"Unless she's an evil faery," Rosamund put in.

All of them turned to her. Phillip's eyes widened a bit. She would have missed it if she hadn't been looking at him. Jeffrey's brows rose in question.

"An evil faery? Phillip, have you been telling tales again?" Jeffrey didn't bother to hide the smirk on his face as he reached for another oatcake.

"Take it easy on those," Charles snapped. "We have to ration."

Jeffrey frowned at his brother as he began gathering the food and wrapping it up once again.

Before Phillip could answer, Rosamund said, "He told me of an evil faery who placed a curse on a baby girl. That she would prick her finger on a thorn and fall into a forever sleep."

Again, they all stared at her as if she were something of an enigma. Jeffrey swallowed the oatcake he'd been eating. Phillip paced the small camp. Charles busied himself with putting the food away into the saddle bags.

"What?" she asked. "Did I say something wrong?"

"You told her that story, did you?" Jeffrey said, looking at Phillip.

Phillip remained devoid of expression as he continued to pace the confines of the camp. "She doesn't know everything."

Confusion flickered through her followed by irritation. "What does that mean?"

"I think you should tell her the truth." Jeffrey brushed crumbs from his hands and gave his friend a pointed look.

"She didn't even know we were betrothed until recently," Phillip said.

"That does pose a problem," Jeffrey replied.

"Would you please stop talking about me as if I weren't here," Rosamund snapped, her ire rising.

Phillip halted, his apprehensive gaze landing on her. Something about that look sent alarm jingling through her, setting her nerves on a raw edge. Her gut clenched, twisted into a tight knot.

"Well?" she demanded.

"Tell her, Phillip. She deserves to know."

After a moment of indecision, Phillip at last nodded. Then he moved to sit next to her, turning to her.

"When I was six years old, my parents and I traveled to Myst Hall to witness the christening of the young princess. You," he said. "You and I were betrothed in an agreement between our fathers to broker a strong alliance because your father, King Stephan, feared Faery, the neighboring kingdom, intended to invade and increase their borders."

Hot pinpricks of fear skittered through her. She didn't like where this was going.

"Your father invited the Fae royals from Faery to the christening as a show of good faith. It was in the hopes they would not invade Stonebridge and leave us be. The royals from four of the Faery Courts arrived in grand fashion. They bestowed upon you faery gifts."

Her brows drew together. "What sort of gifts?"

"Gifts of Fae magic," he said. "One gave you the gift of beauty, charm, and grace. Another strength and bravery. However, your father forgot to invite one of the royals. The queen of the Eternal Court, Queen Rowena," he continued.

Impatience bubbled through her. "What does this have to do with a curse and an evil faery?"

"I'm getting to that," Phillip said, trying to temper her irritation.

By now, Charles joined them in the small circle. He sat on the ground next to his brother. Firelight flickered over his face. Both of them listened to the story as Phillip continued.

"Queen Rowena was so angry she was forgotten she bestowed her gift upon you."

"And what gift was that?" she asked.

"Before the sun sets on your eighteenth birthday, you will prick your finger on the thorn of a rose and die."

The blood drained from her head in a whoosh so fast, she saw black pinpricks dancing in her vision. She looked away from him, peering down at her clasped fingers in her lap. Her heart raced as a dizziness swept over her. And suddenly, she understood why there were no roses in the castle gardens and why her father was adamant there never would be. He was trying to protect her from pricking her finger on a thorn. As the lightheadedness enveloped her, a wave of panic washed over her. She pitched forward, her head in her hands. If she were able to walk, she would have stormed off. As it was, she had to remain in place.

"I think you better finish the story, Phillip," Jeffrey said.

"Finish the story?" Her words were muffled against her hands.

"There was one Fae royal who had not given you her gift," he said, quickly. "She changed the curse to make you fall into a deep sleep, rather than die."

She lifted her head, pinned him with her fiery gaze. "Because that's so much better."

"Rose—"

"I said don't call me that. No one calls me that. Not even my mother," she snapped. "My birthday is the day after tomorrow."

"I know," he said.

"It is?" Jeffrey asked, surprise etching his words.

"And I intend to protect you," Phillip said, ignoring Jeffrey.

"From pricking my finger on a thorn?" She almost laughed. "How do you intend to do that, oh gallant prince?"

Jeffrey and Charles both laughed. Phillip glowered at them.

To Rosamund, he said, "I intend to keep you safe however I must."

"That's very sweet of you, but I don't need your protection." She gave a pointed look to Jeffrey and Charles. "Or anyone's."

"Rose—"

"I *said* stop calling me that!"

"I think she means it," Jeffrey said.

"You stay out of this," Phillip growled.

Jeffrey held his hands up as if in surrender.

"How do I know you're telling the truth?" she demanded. "My parents told me none of this."

Deep down, she knew it was the truth, but she couldn't help but challenge Phillip's story.

"They also didn't tell you that we were betrothed until a few days ago," he pointed out.

And she hated that he knew that. She stared down at her hands, her fingers clamped together to keep them from shaking with her rage, her fear, her shock.

"I tell you true, princess," he said, his voice soft. "There is no reason for me to lie."

He was right, of course, but the truth still stung.

"Why didn't you tell me all this before? When you told me of the evil faery?"

"I don't know," he said and he sounded as though he meant it. "I guess because I was afraid you wouldn't believe me."

All of this was a lot to take. That he was Prince Phillip, hiding from his true identity like she was. That she was cursed to prick her finger on a thorn and fall into a deep sleep. That there was an evil faery somewhere out there that hated an innocent child that much to curse her. Just to spite her father.

"I should have told you sooner," he added.

"It's all right," she said but she wasn't sure it *was* all right. "I understand why you did it."

"I think we should head back to Myst Hall in the morning."

A stabbing pain of horror went through her. She refused to look at him as hot tears burned the backs of her eyes. Though she didn't want to, she nodded agreement.

"I agree," she said, her voice weak. She scooted down into the bedroll and pulled her cloak over her. "Now, I'd like to go to sleep."

There was a long moment of silence, then Phillip said, "Good night, princess."

CHAPTER 20

Rosamund couldn't sleep. It was almost a relief when morning finally dawned. She peered up at the sky and watched it lighten from inky black to indigo. Despair flickered through her at the thought of returning to Myst Hall.

You don't have to go, a voice whispered in her ear.

A strange voice. A voice she had not heard before. She sat up, listening, but all she heard was faint birdsong in the distance as the world came awake. A quick glance at the others, but they were all sleeping. The voice she heard was distinctly female.

Take the map. Go to the dragon's cave. Find the treasure, the voice said.

She pressed cold, shaking fingers against her lips. "I cannot go alone," she whispered to no one.

Find the treasure. Free yourself from a life of drudgery.

Could she? Could she find the treasure? And if she did, would it really free her from her life as a princess? Perhaps so. She would have the means to go anywhere, do anything, be anyone. She could change her name. Blend in as a commoner.

Take the map, the voice whispered again.

She nodded, as if to agree. Yes. Take the map. Find the treasure. Change her life.

She flexed her foot to test it. There was still a bit of soreness, but she was able to pull on the boot. As she sat in her bedroll, she glanced from Phillip to Jeffrey to Charles. All three of them were still sleeping. Good.

She pushed to her feet, and winced at the ache in her left ankle. Ignoring it, though, she managed first one step, then another. It was uncomfortable at best but she had to fight through the pain. She took a step toward the horses, eying the rolled-up map stuck in the saddle bag lying on the ground. Then she paused to glance back at the sleeping men. They hadn't moved.

Another step and another and she was at the discarded saddle bag. She held her breath as she crouched and slipped the map from it. Triumphant, she clutched it in her hand and rose. Her nerves were on edge, but she managed to get the map. Now, she had to saddle her horse and get out of camp as silent as possible.

"Highness, I'd like to know what you're doing."

Jeffrey's voice behind her startled her. She emitted a tiny yelp as she turned. Her heart fluttered wildly as she came face to face with him. He glanced down at the map in her hand and then back up at her. Finally, she pulled herself together and lifted her head a bit in defiance.

"It's none of your concern," she said, keeping her voice low so as not to wake the others.

"Phillip intends to return to Myst Hall. I intend to make sure he does that. *With you*," he said.

He reached for the map but she snatched it away and stepped back onto her weak ankle. She whimpered and stumbled into her horse who snorted annoyance and sidestepped a little to counteract her fall. It took her a minute to regain her footing, but she managed with as much grace as possible.

"I'm not going back," she said, defiant.

Surprise flickered through his eyes. "But—"

"I *won't*," she added.

"What's going on here?" Phillip's sleepy voice interrupted her escape attempt and their discussion.

Frustration edged through her. With him awake, her chances of leaving went to nothing.

Jeffrey stepped aside to face Phillip as he rose from his bedroll. Their eyes collided. He noticed the map clutched in her hand right away.

"Rose?" he queried.

Despite her repeated requests for him not to call her that, he continued to insist. She clenched her jaw as her cheeks burned with the fierce heat of her frustration. The evidence in her hand was all the information he needed to figure out what she was up to. He approached her slowly, as if she were a skittish foal about to bolt. His hands were extended as if in surrender.

"What are you doing with that?" He eyed the map.

"I'm leaving with it," she said, sounding strong and sure.

"You're not going after the dragon's treasure, are you?" Jeffrey asked, incredulous.

Behind them, Charles yawned and stretched. He took in the scene before him and got to his feet, curiosity glinting in his eyes. A sense of unease washed over her as she continued to clutch the map. They were going to talk her out of going and take her back home and then she would still have to marry Phillip.

"That's exactly what she's going to do," Phillip said with a quirk of a grin. There was a hint of admiration in his voice. "Isn't it?"

"It is." She refused to back down.

"She's braver than she looks," Jeffrey remarked.

"I think she's amazing," Charles added.

Phillip lifted one dark brow. "So do I."

Impatience flickered through her as she continued to clutch the map. "I'm leaving with the map."

Without waiting for an answer, she turned toward her horse. The saddle rested on the ground beside her mare. She eyed it with some dismay wishing she had managed to get it on the horse before they awoke.

"I'm sorry, princess, I can't allow you to do that," Phillip said. She started to reply when he added, "Not without a proper escort."

"But Phillip—" Jeffrey said.

Phillip held up his hand to silence his friend's objection. Charles had a wide grin on his youthful face.

"I cannot in good conscience let her go without me," Phillip said. Though he addressed Jeffrey, his gaze never left hers. "It would be unchivalrous."

"I can take care of myself," Rosamund snapped.

"I'm sure you can. But are you prepared to face the dragon?" he asked.

"Not to mention highwaymen or any other manner of men or creatures on the road," Jeffrey added.

Her confidence was starting to melt a little hearing that. "Highwaymen? And what other creatures are there?"

"Trolls, goblins, take your pick," Phillip added. "We've seen them all on our travels."

It was almost enough to make her change her mind and go home. Almost.

"So, I think what his highness believes is that, under the circumstances, we should accompany you," Jeffrey said.

Phillip gave him a sideways glance. "We?"

"You're not getting rid of me that easily," he said. "I made a promise to your mother. I intend to keep that promise. After we go on this quest of hers, we're all going to Myst Hall." He gave her a pointed look that said she didn't have a say in the matter.

"Well, then, it seems it's settled. Charles, saddle the horses," Phillip said.

"Why do I always have to saddle the horses?" he complained.

"Because you're the youngest and that's how it goes," Jeffrey said. He returned to the small camp and started rolling up his bedroll.

Phillip took a step closer to her, though, that smile still on his face. He dropped his voice so the others wouldn't hear him. "Are you sure about this, princess?"

Her nerves were on the edge of a knife. She looked down at the rolled-up map still clutched in her hand and thought about everything she'd done to get to this point. Jeffrey said she was brave, but was she? Perhaps she was mad to even think about going after a dragon and its treasure. But there was something deep inside her that told her she had to go.

"I may never get another chance to have an adventure." As she said it, she looked up at him through her lashes.

Understanding lined his handsome face. His smile faded. Perhaps he was realizing they shared the same fate. That they were bound to each other and their futures were entwined. Like it or not, their wedding awaited at Myst Hall.

"What about the curse?" he asked.

It was a valid question. Her father had removed every rosebush from the royal gardens and even the surrounding castle grounds. She had never seen a rosebush in real life. Only in pictures.

"I suppose I'll have to make sure I don't go near any rosebushes." She handed him the map then. "Here. You should take charge of this."

Surprised, he took it from her. "You don't want to lead us there?"

She flushed, hot. "In truth, I'm terrible at reading maps. It's best if you lead us."

He chuckled. "As you wish, princess."

"While you two were conversing in secret, I broke down camp and Charles readied the horses," Jeffrey said, sounding annoyed. "Shall we get on the road?"

Phillip gave her a questioning glance. "Shall we, princess?"

Nodding, she said, "I am ready."

Rowena held the All-Seeing Eye in her palm and used her magic to make it come to life to watch the prince and princess. They had almost turned back, which she could not allow to happen. She needed them to go to the dragon's lair so the princess would face her fate at last. She used a bit of her Faery magic to encourage the princess to go on the quest. Much to her surprise and annoyance, the men decided to go with her. One more night and then her birthday would be upon her. Rowena's plan would at last come to fruition.

Smiling, she clutched her fingers around the green orb, snuffing out its magic. It was almost time for the princess to meet her doom.

Chapter 21

They traveled west through the Mystwood Forest, going deeper and deeper into the trees. Before they departed, Phillip consulted the map and committed their direction to memory. He and Jeffrey chatted about their previous adventures. She rode behind them with Charles next to her. She was aware of the sideways glances he gave her as they traveled.

Through their conversations, she learned Jeffrey was the son of a duke. The duke being the king's brother. The two of them had grown up together with them spending most of their time in Haven Castle. Jeffrey would inherit his father's title while Charles, being the second born, would not.

"You're to marry the prince, then," Charles said.

She was aware he was making small talk. "I am."

"But neither of you wish to marry the other." A statement, rather than a question.

"It appears so," she replied.

All the while she kept her gaze forward watching as Phillip and Jeffrey shared a laugh. There was such life in the prince as he tossed his head back. He was handsome, certainly. He made her feel safe when they were together. He promised to keep her from pricking her finger on a thorn before the sun set on her birthday tomorrow. There was something sweet and endearing about that. It was difficult for her to think of him as her future husband.

But why shouldn't she? Their parents had agreed to the betrothal when they were both children. She doubted they would break that betrothal.

Would it be so terrible to marry Phillip? She asked herself this more than once over the last few hours as they rode.

"What if there was another suitor?" Charles asked.

His question broke into her thoughts. Startled, she met his gaze and saw the look of hope buried deep within his eyes.

"Another suitor?" she asked.

"Give it up, brother. The princess is spoken for," Jeffrey said over his shoulder.

Charles flushed a deep red to the roots of his hair and turned away, his eyes forward. His brother clearly had no qualms about embarrassing him in front of her.

"That's not very nice of you," she said, chastising him.

"It's all right, your highness." Charles sounded so defeated he made her heart ache.

A low growl from somewhere in the forest cut off any response she might have had. Phillip held up a hand for them to halt. Her heart pounded as the growl sounded again, echoing through the forest.

"What is it?" Her voice was a breath of a whisper.

Phillip pulled out his sword and held it. Jeffrey did the same. Each of them glanced around the area as another guttural growl sounded again. This one was followed by a thunderous rumbling of the ground. Phillip and Jeffrey exchanged a look, and then in unison, both dismounted.

"Charles, take the princess to safety," Phillip ordered, clutching his sword.

"To safety? Where?" She surveyed her surroundings trying to find someplace safe to hide from whatever doom was upon them.

"Come with me, princess." Charles turned his horse and headed back the way they came.

She hesitated a moment too long. Suddenly the giant crashed through the trees, felling them as he went. The two horses fled. The thunderous noise they'd heard was that of his huge footsteps. He was as tall as the trees with dark round eyes. His skin was a sickly pallor and he wore nothing but a tattered cloth about his hips. When he growled again, he showed off stump teeth. He took a swipe at Jeffrey who dropped and rolled out of the way.

"What—"

"Troll! Princess, come!" Charles shouted, cutting her off.

Phillip went into action as the beastly thing headed for Jeffrey, reaching for him. He swiped his sword in an arc, slicing it across the back of the legs.

When she still failed to move, Charles reached over and grabbed her reins, giving them a tug.

"Come on," he said.

Then he turned to flee. She did the same. As she did, she saw the large hand come down and swipe Charles off his mount. He went flying into the trees, crashing against one and tumbling to the ground. She gasped.

"Charles!"

That was enough to garner the troll's unwanted attention. Black narrow eyes landed on her making all her limbs shake. She gripped the reins so tight, her hands ached. The troll took two giant steps and was upon her in an instant. Her horse bucked. Though she tried to hang on, she knew from experience it was better to let go. She tumbled to the ground as her horse galloped away. Without looking back, she crawled over the forest floor. Thick underbrush was ahead. She headed there hoping it would hide her from the beast.

Behind her, the troll cried out. Despite her better judgement, she glanced over her shoulder to see Jeffrey and Phillip had both attacked. No longer interested in her, the troll turned his attention back to the two men.

Nearby, Charles groaned. She stopped and turned toward him. He was on the ground at the base of a tree. Still on her hands and knees, she quickly crawled to his side. He had a terrible gash on his head. She pulled him into her lap, wrapping her arms around his upper torso.

"Shhh," she said. "Don't move. I'm here."

"Princess?" he muttered. "The troll...?"

"Looks like your brother and Phillip have everything in hand."

It was a lie, she knew, as she glanced up to see them fighting the large beastly thing. The troll hit Phillip so hard, he tumbled to the ground, his sword flying out of his hand. She bit her lip to keep from crying out. She eyed the sword lying out of his reach as Jeffrey went after the troll again. Every attempt he made to strike was outmaneuvered.

"Stay here," she whispered. "Stay quiet. I'll be back."

Gently, she placed Charles back on the ground. He groaned but didn't try to fight her or talk her out of it. Still on her hands and knees, she crawled toward Phillip's sword. He managed to get to his feet, shaking his head to clear it, and then pulled out his dagger. He charged the troll while the beast was busy with Jeffrey.

As she reached the sword, Phillip plunged the dagger into the back of the troll's leg. He cried out, an ear-piercing shout that rattled the treetops as he flung his large head back. He stumbled to the left, then the right. Phillip only had time to shout a warning before the troll fell, a descent that took out numerous trees on the way down.

Jeffrey jumped out to the way as it crashed with a resounding thud. Rosamund gripped Phillip's sword in her hand and jumped to her feet. The troll rolled to his stomach, trying to get back to his feet. Without thinking, she charged, clutching the sword in both hands.

The troll pushed up to his hands and knees. Phillip's dagger still stuck out of his thigh which oozed black blood.

"Rose!"

Phillip shouted her name as she came face to face with the troll. He growled, showing off nasty teeth, then reached for her with a large, meaty hand. Long fingers wrapped around her torso and hoisted her up into the air.

Sucking in a sharp breath, she used every ounce of energy and strength she had to shove the sword right into the troll's left eye. Furious, he reared back crying out in pain as he released her. She, at least, had enough thought to let go of the hilt as she fell, landing on the ground hard enough to jam her elbow.

The troll crashed against the ground. He flinched one last time, gave out a pitiful moan, and then was dead.

Phillip was at her side in an instant, scooping her into his arms and cradling her against his chest. She heard the wild beat of his heart hammering against her ear. He clutched her tight, as though he might never let her go.

"Are you all right?"

"Yes," she said. For a moment, their eyes met and her heart did a funny thud followed by a fluttering in her gut.

"What you did was..." he began.

"Incredibly stupid," she finished.

He grinned as a low chuckle rumbled through his chest. "Perhaps."

"Brave, indeed, princess," Jeffrey said, sounding impressed as he approached. "Even though you could have been injured or, worse, killed."

She pushed out of Phillip's arms and scrambled away from him. Her elbow throbbed with an almost unbearable pain that went all the way to her shoulder. She tried to ignore it as she got to her feet.

"But I wasn't," she said, brushing the leaves and grass from her pants.

A faint groan sounded. She gasped as she glanced in the direction of Charles. She tried to hurry over to him, but her ankle was still giving her trouble. Instead, it was more of a hobble. As she neared him, he sat up, clutching his head and looking pale. He moaned again.

"Let me help you," she said as she reached down to grasp his arm.

Jeffrey was there on the other side of him. Together, they hoisted Charles to his feet. The gash on his head continued to bleed.

"That's a nasty gash on your head. We better see to it," Jeffrey said.

"Where are the horses?" Phillip asked, glancing around.

They all stood within the destroyed forest, but the horses were nowhere to be found.

"The troll scared them off," Jeffrey said. "Here's hoping we can find them and not have to continue on foot."

Charles emitted a faint grumble of despair. Rosamund felt the same way. She would be unable to continue on foot with her sore ankle. Phillip retrieved his sword from the dead troll. Black blood coated the once-shiny steel. Frowning, he managed to scrape off most of the blood on one of the felled trees.

"I'll find them," Phillip said.

Before anyone could object, he was off through the forest, whistling and calling for them. Jeffrey walked Charles over to a fallen tree and lowered him down. Charles expelled a long breath as though he were exhausted as he leaned back and closed his eyes.

"My head hurts," he muttered.

Jeffrey ripped a piece of his tunic at the bottom edge. When he had a decent sized cloth he reached for his brother, placing the cloth on the bleeding gash. Rosamund limped toward them.

"Here, let me." She held out her hand for the cloth.

"No need, princess. I can—"

"Jeffrey, give it to her and go find the other horses. She's a prettier nursemaid than you are," Charles said without opening his eyes.

Shock registered on his face as he glanced from his brother and then to Rosamund. He removed the bloodied cloth and handed it to her.

"He really must have hit his head hard," he muttered.

She took it and lowered herself to the ground next to Charles as Jeffrey lumbered off to find the other two horses. With a gentle hand, she dabbed the cloth along the gash to clear away the blood.

"I think you surprised your brother," she said, a hint of humor in her voice.

"What I said was true." He winced as she dabbed at the worst of the cut. One eye cracked open as he looked at her. "You are far prettier than he is."

It was hard not to grin at that. "You flatter me, my lord."

"You don't believe me?"

She considered this a moment as she continued to dab away the blood. She had never really thought of herself as beautiful or pretty or anything other than plain. Her mother, though, had all the looks and she wished she was half as regal and lovely as her. Thinking of her mother sent a pang of homesickness through her.

She halted her hand, thinking of her home and her parents and wondering what happened to the soldiers who had come looking for her. Had they given up and returned to the castle? Or were they still out there searching for her?

Her mother must be beside herself with worry. Rosamund also thought of the visiting royals—Phillip's parents—and recalled how kind Queen Adele was to her when she arrived. For the first time, since wondered what would happen when they returned together. Would their parents be overjoyed? Furious? Both?

"You should," Charles continued, unaware of her inner strife. "You were touched by Fae magic."

She snorted. "And cursed by Fae magic if what Phillip said is true." She finished dabbing his forehead. "The cut isn't as bad as it looked. I think you'll be fine."

"That's good to hear."

When she sat back, she met his gaze. There she saw admiration and something akin to affection. A faint smile crossed his lips.

"Charles, you should know—"

"You don't have to say it." The affection faded from his face. "I know the truth of it. You will marry Phillip. The alliance between Myst and Woodhaven will be sealed and the borders of Stone-bridge will be strong and safe from those Fae royals."

She settled on the ground next to him, leaning her back against the fallen tree. She pulled off her boot, flexing her foot to work out her sore ankle. The throbbing of her elbow had dissipated to a dull ache.

"Is there a threat from Faery?" she asked.

"I can't say. If there is, it's from the Fae royal who was forgotten and not invited to your christening."

"A Fae royal would hold a grudge for eighteen years?" It was more of a rhetorical question. She didn't expect an answer.

"People have held grudges for far longer for far less."

She supposed he was right. As she sat there, wondering if Phillip and Jeffrey would return with the horses, she could not ignore the apprehension shifting through her. Tomorrow was her eighteenth birthday. Tomorrow, she was supposed to prick her finger on a thorn and fall into a forever slumber.

She hoped she wouldn't run into any thorns in her quest to find the dragon's treasure.

Rowena cackled as she peered through the All-Seeing Eye. "Yes, dear sweet child. A Fae royal *would* hold a grudge for eighteen years. And, soon, you will feel my wrath."

The girl's birthday was tomorrow.

Tomorrow vengeance would be hers.

Tomorrow the girl would prick her finger on a thorn.

Tomorrow the girl would die.

Chapter 22

Phillip found his and Jeffrey's horse grazing peacefully in a nearby meadow. Well, nearby wasn't exactly accurate. It was more of a hike. He tied Jeffrey's horse to his and made his way back as the sun dipped toward the horizon.

As he did, he couldn't help but think of all the strange happenings since meeting Rosamund. He thought of the soldiers from Myst Hall who found them in town a few days ago and how easily they seemed to have given up searching for her. He wondered why. She was a princess, after all. More soldiers should be swarming the forest by now. But they weren't.

And then there was the old hag, Olga and her mysterious cabin had conveniently appeared within the woods when they needed food and shelter. When she mentioned the dragon and its treasure, a thrum of excitement went through him almost immediately. It was unlike anything he had ever felt before. As though he had a sudden need to find this treasure and live out a boyhood fantasy that he never knew he had.

Then there was the troll that seemed to pop up out of nowhere. Trolls did not normally roam these woods. It was merely something he said to frighten the princess a little. To make sure she needed him to protect her.

Turns out, she didn't need him to protect her at all. She had wielded his sword as though she were a master. He'd watched in fascinated horror as she stuck the thing in the eye, killing it.

Even so, where had the troll come from?

It was early nightfall as he neared the makeshift camp that had popped up. He was relieved to see the other two horses had not escaped and were running wild somewhere deep in the forest.

"Should you go after him?" Rosamund asked. She sat on the ground next to Charles, clutching her elbows. "It's almost dark."

Jeffrey was perched on a rock opposite them. In between them, a crackling fire.

"He'll be fine," Jeffrey said in his most bored and annoyed voice.

"Will he?" Phillip called out as he approached.

He caught sight of Rosamund as she sat straighter. Her face lit up when she saw him. It was clear she was glad to see him which did something to his insides. He paused to analyze that for a moment and realized it was happiness.

Yes, he was happy to see her, too. Though he was not too happy to see her sitting next to Charles who swooned over her since the moment he met her.

"About time you showed up." Jeffrey stopped what was he was doing to give him a stern look. "We were beginning to think you left us."

He noticed Rosamund got to her feet and limped toward him. She was favoring her twisted ankle still. Other than that, she appeared to be unscathed from the troll attack.

"Only Jeffrey thought that," she said, correcting Jeffrey and giving Phillip a smile. "I'm glad you're back."

His heart stuttered with her words and for a moment, he forgot they were promised to one another. For a moment, she was merely a lovely young maid who currently caught his attention.

Phillip came to a halt and dismounted. "It was a bit of a hike to find the horses. They made it to a far meadow."

"Charles, come tend the horses," Jeffrey ordered.

"Leave him be. He's injured," Rosamund snapped, fire flashing in her eyes.

A look of surprise flickered over his friend's face. He was unaccustomed to being told what to do.

"Perhaps you should take care of the horses, Jeffrey," Phillip suggested.

With some reluctance, he took the reins and led the horses away to remove their saddles and feed them. That left him with the princess, something with which he was not opposed. When she hooked her arm with his, shock went through him.

"Were you bored without my company, princess?" He made a point to glance down at her stocking foot. "You're still limping."

"I'll be fine."

Even as she said it, she leaned into him to keep as much weight off her foot as possible. If they were in any other place, under any other circumstances, he would whisk her into his arms and carry her away from these two. Perhaps find a secluded camp of their own so that he could properly woo her.

The moment the thought crossed his mind, he shoved it away. He had to remind himself she was no ordinary tavern wench. She was much more than that and deserved to be treated better.

"I think you took poor Jeffrey aback," Phillip said, glancing his friend's way. He was frowning as he tended the horses.

Rosamund clutched his arm tighter. "Charles needs rest after hitting his head."

"Do I detect a note of affection for him?" He was teasing her even though he shouldn't. He was also aware of the bit of jealousy that had surfaced when he saw them sitting together.

"Nothing more than friendship," she replied, her tone even. She wasn't going to let him to rile her. "Though I daresay he seems to like me more than I like him."

She cut him a glance through her lashes and gave him a wicked smile. As if she sensed his jealousy and wanted to make sure he knew it. He lifted a brow.

"Does he now?"

"He said I was touched by Fae magic."

When they came to a halt, he turned to her. "You were. But you sound as though you don't believe me."

She glanced away, her gaze on something in the distance. "I don't know if I do. My parents certainly never told me that story."

"Your parents also never told you that you were betrothed," he pointed out.

Nodding, she said, "That's true."

She released his arm and turned her face into the gentle wind. Her scent wafted to him. For the first time, he noticed she smelled faintly of roses and lilacs. Her nickname, Rose, seemed to fit her so well. The wind lifted wisps of hair from her neck and the side of her face. Her braid had nearly come undone from the troll attack, leaving tendrils to drift around her head.

"When I was a little girl, my father had every rosebush in the kingdom removed and outlawed. I didn't understand then why he did it, but I do now. He wanted to protect me." Her gaze met his. "He wanted to keep me safe. Part of me wants to believe that the truth is because the faery cursed me. The other part of me wants to scoff at the very idea."

He tipped his head to the side in question, his eyes searching hers. She had delicate features and the most amazing green eyes he had ever seen. Her full lips demanded he kiss her, but somehow, he managed to resist.

"Which part of you wants to believe?" he asked.

"That the curse is real."

He had no words for that, so he merely nodded. He watched her intently as she pondered his words. She chewed on a corner of her lip.

"I don't believe you'd lie to me," she added.

"I didn't nor will I."

Suddenly, she turned to face him and clutched his hand, gripping it in her ice cold one. "Then tell me true. Do you wish to marry me? Do you wish for our kingdoms to be united? Because my father believes there is a threat from Faery to the east, that they will invade."

Phillip was momentarily taken aback by that and he floundered for an answer. His mouth had gone dry as he thought about a future with her. As he looked at her, he tried to decide if there was hope in her eyes that they would marry or if it was dread.

"For the last few years, my father groomed me to become a ruler because someday I would inherit his title. I sat in many council meetings and listened to them discuss this threat from Faery. My father, like I, do not believe there is a threat. They have no interest in our kingdom."

"Then why did my father invite them to the christening?" she demanded.

"I do not know. Only that King Stephan's desire was to unite Myst and Woodhaven and that my father agreed to it with a marriage bond," he said. "It is the way of such things."

She released his hand. Again, she turned from him and peered out into the distance, her expression pensive. She chewed on her lower lip.

"I cannot help but think that something is pushing us together."

"What do you mean?" he asked.

"I mean despite every thought I have that what I'm doing is wrong, that it's hurting my kingdom and my family…I cannot seem to quell the desire to find this dragon and its treasure."

A prickling sensation went through him and his stomach lurched. He dropped his voice. "I have felt the same."

When she looked at him, he saw the fear and worry in her eyes. "You have?"

"Though I know we should return to Myst Hall, I also know I cannot ignore the need to find this treasure. To hunt this dragon. And that I must not let you out of my sight." He reached for her hand, clutched it in his. Her fingers were still cold. "The troll attack should not have happened."

"What do you mean?" She tilted her head to one side, pursing her lips.

He tugged her closer, glancing around the tiny camp. Jeffrey was still busy with the horses. Charles was resting against the fallen tree with his eyes closed. Still, he dropped his voice so only she heard.

"Trolls do not frequent these woods," he added.

"Then someone sent the troll to attack us," she said.

"And that someone wanted the troll to remove Jeffrey and Charles from our traveling party. The troll went for Jeffrey first."

She squeezed his hand. "Yes, and then you."

"But only because I retaliated. It attacked me in self-defense."

Her mind was working as she tried to make sense of all he said. "And then came after Charles."

He nodded.

"Which means whoever sent the troll wants to make sure only the two of us make it to the dragon's cave."

It was something he, too, had thought of. "I believe so."

"And the old woman in the cabin…she made sure to give you the map to the cave, to entice you to go after it," she added. She pressed her free hand to her lips. Her hand was shaking. "And that night, I had the overwhelming urge to go after the dragon and its treasure as well."

"I believe there are magical forces at work here," he said. "Magical forces pushing us together and toward the dragon and its treasure."

"But why?" she whispered and then her eyes widened as the realization smacked into her with the force of a battering ram. "Tomorrow is my eighteenth birthday."

He had no response other than a nod. He remembered all too well the curse that was placed upon her as a baby. That before the sun set on her eighteenth birthday, she would prick her finger.

"What do we do?" she asked. "Do we keep going?"

"I think we have to," he said. "If only to release us from whatever spell is driving us."

Silence stretched between them. After a long moment, she said, "Well, then," her words slow and quiet, "let us hope we find no roses."

CHAPTER 23

Sleep did not come easily for Rosamund. She lay curled on her side in the bedroll, staring at the fire as the flames flickered and died down into nothing but hot embers. She was still staring at it, not having slept a wink, when the darkened sky began to lighten with the coming dawn.

Soon, the men would rise, and they would pack up the camp and be on their way. Possibly to her doom.

Today was her birthday. She didn't feel as though she had aged another year.

As she lay there, listening to the world come alive around her, she thought of her mother and how she must be feeling this morning. Likely missing her and wondering when or if she'd return home. She envisioned her mother pacing the length of her chamber. Would she have tried to occupy her mind by convening her sewing circle? Or would she have banished them from her chamber to be alone with her grief and her agony?

Then Rosamund thought of her father who had removed every rose from the castle grounds in an act of love and protection. How he had made sure she never ventured out without an escort of castle guards. She wondered what he was doing now. If he was spewing his wrath to all those who were supposed to guard the castle. She could almost hear his voice now, chastising them for allowing her to slip out and disappear. Though he was generally a calm man, when he was upset or angry, his wrath knew no bounds and all those in his path were victim to it.

What a horrible daughter she was by sneaking off into the night.

"Rose?"

Her whispered name startled her. She sat up quickly to see Phillip in the bedroll next to her, his eyes nothing but dark orbs in the half light. He put a finger to his lips. She nodded as she tried to slow her rapidly beating heart. Then he waved her to follow him.

Crouched low, he walked to the horses. His steps were virtually silent as he made his way, leaving behind his bedroll. She quickly reached for her boots but decided not to put them on yet. Clutching them, she crawled out of the bedroll and stood. With a quick glance around the small camp, she saw Charles and Jeffrey were still sleeping.

Ahead of her, Phillip gave a frantic wave for her to hurry.

In her stocking feet, she hurried to the horses doing her best to be as silent as he was. When she was close enough, he took her hand and pulled her to him, wrapping an arm around her shoulders to whisper in her ear.

"I have one horse saddled," he said. "We'll leave together on that."

"Leave?" She blinked up at him, her eyes wide.

The way he held her to him made her heart do a strange little dance. There was a swooping in the pit of her stomach and, for a moment, she thought she saw starlight in his eyes. His gaze flickered from her eyes to her lips and back again. The way he looked at her sent a shuddering thrill through her. She thought he might kiss her.

A desperate need for him to kiss her swept through her.

"To find the treasure," he said at last. And then released her.

Disappointment flooded her when he didn't kiss her. He made a motion for her to come closer. She held up her boots and he suppressed a laugh. He gave her a nod as if to say hurry.

She balanced on her good ankle and pulled the boot onto her other one. Then she wobbled when she tried to balance on the other foot. Pain lanced through her sore ankle, objecting to the movement. He was there in an instant, though, making sure she didn't tumble to the ground. He placed his body behind hers, giving her something to lean against.

Her heart did that silly little tumble again as she glanced up at him, giving him a weak smile. Did he know what he was doing to her? Likely not.

Leveraging her weight against him, she managed to pull on the second boot. Then he turned to her, placing his hands on her waist. He paused, their eyes meeting again making her heart thud. She was sure he could see the frantic beat of her pulse. One corner of his mouth lifted in a quirk of a grin.

"Happy birthday, princess," he whispered.

He remembered. Something about that endeared him to her and she flushed hot.

"Thank you."

Then he helped hoist her onto the horse. He settled into the saddle in front of her. She wrapped her arms around his waist as he gripped the reins and gave a low click of his tongue and then they were at a brisk trot. Heading away from the camp to seek the dragon's treasure.

She glanced back one last time to see Jeffrey and Charles still fast asleep. Ahead, the sun peeked over the horizon and morning dawned.

"Do you really think there will be treasure?" she asked.

"I guess we'll find out, won't we?" he replied.

"It seems silly to think there is a cave with hidden treasure," she added.

"I agree, it does. But shouldn't we at least check?"

Despite her reservations, she smiled. "We should."

But she knew, as he did, neither of them had a choice. They were both compelled to continue onward to the mysterious dragon's cave.

"Won't Jeffrey be angry when he wakes to find us gone?" she asked.

"He will, but he'll get over it."

"Will he come after us?" she asked.

He was silent a moment before he finally answered. "Yes, Jeffrey is an excellent tracker. He can track anything or anyone."

"That's how he was able to find you in the woods, then," she said.

"It is."

"So, it means we have to hurry to get to the dragon's cave before he finds us."

"Exactly."

But she wondered. Was it because he didn't want to share the treasure with him? Or was there some other reason? She, herself, had her own reasons. Despite the guilt running through her, she was still determined to take what she could from the treasure and make a new life somewhere else.

"How long will it take us to get there?" she asked.

"You ask a lot of questions." There was a smile in his voice as he said it.

"I'm curious," she said.

"We should be there this afternoon."

This afternoon, as the day waned and sunset neared. The curse sprang to her mind. She only had a few more hours left to avoid roses and thorns. Hopefully she would make it without pricking her finger.

They rode all day until the sun started to dip toward the horizon. He kept a good pace, only slowing the horse over rough terrain. When exhaustion from being up most of the night finally caught up to her, she managed to doze.

"Rose, look!"

Her head snapped up, her neck aching. She stretched as tall as was possible to peer over his shoulder as he brought the horse to a halt.

Though the trees were still dense here, there was a break where there was stone rockface. At the sight of it, her breath hitched in surprise and a gasp escaped her lips. A jolt of excitement skittered down her spine, sending shivers of anticipation dancing along her skin. The sight of it ignited a fierce eagerness propelling her forward with her continued determination.

"The cave?" she asked.

"Let's find out."

His voice quivered with a mix of enthusiasm and anticipation. He slid out of the saddle, then turned with his arms outstretched to help her down. She swung her good leg over but didn't quite calculate the distance correctly and practically fell off the horse. Phillip was there, though, catching her in his arms.

They came nose to nose. Her breath caught in her throat as she peered up at him. It was as though there was an eager anticipation emanating off him. It was difficult for her deny she felt the same. She could not deny the yearning sweeping through her, trying to melt away her resolve.

"This is the second time you've landed in my arms."

His voice was low and dark and floated over her, sending her senses reeling. He was so close his breath fanned her face as he spoke. So close, his lips were a breath away from hers.

"I'll try not to make a habit of it." Much to her dismay, her voice trembled.

The smile in his eyes contained a sensuous flame.

"Pity." Then he released her to turn toward the rockface. "This has to be the dragon's cave, don't you think?"

Was he nervous? Did she knock him off kilter as he did her? She smiled to herself as he spoke.

"As you said, let's find out," she said, nudging him with her elbow.

There was a spark of elation in his eyes as he looked at her and nodded. "Right."

He took her by the hand, making her heart soar with delight, and led her toward the rockface.

Overhead, there was the unmistakable *whump, whump* of wings. They both paused to look up as the shadow moved across the illuminated sky. The sun had not yet set. Her heart picked up speed.

"We better hurry," he said.

He released her hand and jogged toward the rockface. She hurried after him. As they approached, though, they both saw it was nothing more than rock. No cave. But Rosamund saw there was what appeared to be a well-worn trail to the left and took it.

"I think it's this way," she said.

He followed her. "Don't you think I should lead?"

"Why? Just because you're the man?" she said.

"Well—"

"I'm perfectly capable—"

Her words were cut short by a creature leaping out in front of her. She squealed and stumbled backward, her weak ankle protesting at the sudden movement. The small, big eared creature with a long nose bared its teeth at her, lifting his hands with sharp pointy nails, and then growled.

"Och, did I frighten ye?" he said.

Phillip moved around her, pushing her behind him in a protective gesture. The creature's ears drooped and his face fell as he looked up at Phillip with big, black eyes.

"I didn't mean to frighten the lady. Honest. I thought she was something good to eat."

"Be gone, goblin," Phillip said with a wave of his hand. "There's nothing to eat here."

The goblin peered around Phillip to look at her with huge round eyes. "Forgive me, lady?"

He was hard to resist with him looking at her like that full of longing she would agree. She started to step around Phillip, but he put out his arm to stop her and gave a shake of his head.

"Don't fall for it. He merely wants sympathy."

"I didn't mean no harm!" the goblin wailed. Then threw himself on the ground, covering his head and crying wracking sobs.

"But—" she began.

"No," Phillip said, his tone firm. "He's a trickster."

The goblin continued to wail. "I'm no trickster, sir! I only want to apologize to the lady proper like."

Rosamund started to melt a little, but Phillip's eyes were hard and unrelenting. She glanced from him to the creature squirming with his cries on the ground.

"He wants your sympathy. Then when you give it and get close to him, he'll steal whatever he can off you."

The goblin continued to howl. As she peered at him, an idea formed.

"If I forgive you, will you do you something for me?" she asked.

That dried up the goblin's tears almost immediately. He sat straight up and gave her his full attention.

"Anything for you lady!"

"What are you doing?" Phillip said, his words hissing through his teeth.

"Trust me," she whispered back. Then to the goblin, "You will have my forgiveness if you take us to the dragon's cave."

The goblin stared up at her, sniffed, then wiped snot from his nose. "The dragon's cave?"

"Yes. It's here, isn't it?"

The goblin glanced behind him, then moved closer and dropped his voice. "The dragon's cave is near, yes."

"Can you take us there?" she asked.

"And then you'll forgive me for scaring you?" he asked.

She nodded. "Yes, I will."

"Then follow me! Come! Hurry!" he called over his shoulder as he scurried away.

"Very clever, princess," Phillip said. He motioned her ahead. "After you."

CHAPTER 24

S he hurried after the goblin, who was fast and low to the
ground. She had difficulty keeping up with him. Phillip was
right on her heels. So close she thought she heard his breath as he
did his best to keep up.

The goblin disappeared around a corner. A moment later his
head popped around the side to make sure they still followed.
Satisfied, he was gone again in an instant.

"He's a fast one," Phillip said, out of breath.

She agreed but said nothing as she rounded the corner and came
to a jarring halt. Phillip cursed under his breath as he bumped into
her. Ahead, the goblin hopped from one foot to the other clearly
proud he was able to complete his task. He gestured wildly to the
opening in front of him.

"Here it is, milady. See?"

She stepped next to him and peered into the dark opening of the
cave. "I see."

"I did what you asked. Now will you forgive me?"

Phillip moved to stand next to her, his attention on the cave.
Rosamund nodded.

"I forgive you."

"Thank you!"

Then the goblin's smile turned viscous as he leapt. She emitted a sharp gasp of surprise and stumbled backward, her weak ankle giving way. They crashed to the ground. The goblin was on her in an instant. She put her arms up in defense against his gnashing spiky teeth. Phillip roared something incoherent and seconds later the goblin went flying off her into the trees.

He reached a hand down to her. She grasped it. He pulled her to her feet and wielded his sword in one smooth motion as the goblin reemerged from the trees. Gone was the pleasant expression only to be replaced by the wicked grin. But it faded quickly when he came face to face with the point of Phillip's sword.

"Stay back," Phillip warned.

The goblin frowned. His eyes filled with tears. "I meant no harm, really. I just wanted a taste of the lady."

"Stay back," he repeated and jabbed the sword at the goblin.

He stumbled backward several steps, his eyes wide and round. "But—"

"Be gone. And do not return. For if you do…" He paused, sticking the end of his sword against the goblin's nose. He went crossed-eyed to look at it. "I will make sure you never breathe again."

The goblin held up his hands and backed slowly away until there was a good bit of distance between him and Phillip. Then he scampered back into the trees, disappearing. Phillip stood there a moment, his hand on his sword waiting to see if he returned. The goblin did not. He replaced his sword, then turned to her.

"Are you all right?" he asked.

The goblin's teeth tore through her sleeves, leaving them tattered. Other than that, she sustained no other damage. She nodded.

"You ask me that a lot," she said.

"Because you get yourself into trouble a lot." He winked as he said it. "It's why I'm here to keep you safe."

She grinned. "I'm fine, really."

Relief passed over his face.

"Protecting you is quite the challenge."

Though she knew he jested something inside her quivered. She liked the idea of him protecting her. Still holding her hand, he looked toward the shadowy cave entrance.

"Looks like we found it," he said.

Trepidation edged through her. And yet it was impossible to refuse the call to enter and find out if there was, in fact, a treasure within it.

"Are you sure about this?" he asked.

"No," she admitted. "Yet, I find I cannot resist stepping inside."

He squeezed her hand. "Nor I."

Together, they turned toward the cave and entered.

The darkness pressed all around them. A damp smell accosted her nose. An icy fear skittered up her spine. She edged closer to him as they moved deeper, the light from the mouth of the cave at their backs. It was getting more and more difficult to see.

"We need a torch," she said.

"Yes," he agreed. "I should have..."

His words trailed off. He cut her a glance, then reached for something in the darkness. She was unsure of what he grabbed until he pulled it closer to him. He held a torch.

They exchanged a glance, each knowing what the other was thinking. It was as though the torch was conjured for them. Whoever was pushing them into the cave was listening. He stared at the unlit wick.

"Now, if only we had a way to light it." As he said it, he gave her a pointed look of anticipation, as though waiting for his wish to be granted. His voice echoed through the cavern.

Seconds later, the torch sprang to life, emitting a yellow-orange glow all around them. Again, their eyes met. He lifted one brow in a silent question. Her nerves were on high alert.

"Magic?" she whispered.

"Most definitely," he replied.

Still clutching her hand, he held the torch aloft and led them deeper into the cave. The light flickered off the stone walls. The only sound was that of their footfalls. Rosamund held her breath the farther they went, unable to see much in the murky gloom beyond the light of the torch.

The cave abruptly ended. They came to a halt, facing a wall with no other junctures to lead them anywhere. It was a dead end.

"This can't be all." Her words were laced with frustration. "This cave is not big enough for a dragon. Maybe this is the wrong place."

"This cave is the one marked on the map," he said.

Disappointment flooded her as she peered at the wall in dismay. How could they have been led here only to find nothing? Her hopes of gathering enough treasure to start a new life were completely shattered.

She pushed past him and stood before the wall, looking for any imperceptible crack that would lead them to a secret door or chamber or something. She ran her hands over the roughened stone, pushing here and there.

"What are you doing?" he asked, genuinely perplexed.

"I refuse to believe we were led to a dead end with nothing," she said, and gave the wall a great shove. Nothing happened. "I'm looking for a secret chamber. A lever or something that will open when I push on it and lead us to the treasure. There has to be something—"

"Rose." He said her name softly.

She turned to him to see the disappointment in his eyes and she knew what she was trying to do was folly.

"It's no use," he said.

"But…"

She huffed out a breath and glared at the dead end, willing there to be something more. Something shiny caught her eye near his boot. She reached down to pick it up and realized it was one gold coin. She placed it in her palm and held it out to show him.

"A gold coin," he said, sounding defeated. He took it and held it up, letting the torchlight flicker over the shiny surface. "I suppose that's all that's left then."

She stared at it, her eyes dry and hot with the threat of tears. She swallowed hard to keep her emotions in check. "Yes, I suppose it is."

He held it out to her. "You take it."

"Why?"

"You're the one who found it."

Rosamund took it back from him, her thumb swiping over the smooth surface. She was silly to think she would be able to start over as someone else. Her life was mapped out for her, after all. They would return home. She and Phillip would marry. And that would be the end of her adventures.

Closing the coin in her fist, she looked up at him through her lashes. Would it be so terrible to marry him? He was handsome, after all. He was kind to her even when he didn't know she was a princess and then when he did. Even so, she had to question if it was the magic at work or if that was his true disposition.

"What is it?" he asked, tipping his head to the side.

Realizing she stared, she tore her gaze away and turned back the way they came. Ahead, there was nothing but darkness and shadows.

"I suppose now we should return to Myst Hall."

There was a long moment of silence, as though he, too, contemplated the same thing. He reached for her free hand, taking it in his once more.

"It would be my honor to escort you home, princess."

With a smile, she nodded. "I should like that."

Together, hand in hand, they headed back through the dank cave, toward their future as husband and wife. In her other hand, she still clutched the coin.

"Do you think Jeffrey found us yet?" she asked as they walked.

"I wouldn't be surprised if he was waiting outside the cave when we exit," he said, humor in his voice.

She didn't doubt that either. As the pinprick of light expanded, she realized the sun must be dipping closer to the horizon. Which meant her birthday was nearly over. And that meant she had managed to get through the entire day without pricking her finger. The curse had not come true.

Her steps were a little lighter. Her mood a little happier.

"I'm sorry we didn't find the treasure," Phillip said. "I hope that doesn't ruin your future plans."

Her head snapped in his direction. "Whatever do you mean?"

Phillip gave her a knowing grin. "You *were* planning something, weren't you?"

Rosamund flushed to the roots of her hair and turned away, dislodging her hand from his. "I was not."

"Ah, but you were." There was a smugness in his words.

She increased her speed as she hurried toward the opening.

"Come on, now. You can tell me."

His cajoling was starting to get on her nerves.

"All right, then. If you won't tell me what you were planning to do with the treasure, then I'll tell you my plans," he said.

That caught her attention. She paused and turned to look at him, waiting.

"You had plans?" she asked.

"Certainly. I was going to take enough money to keep me comfortable while I hunted and drank ale."

For a moment, she believed him. And then he gave her wicked grin. She punched him in the arm.

"You weren't," she snapped. Then she turned and hurried toward the exit once more.

"Rose, wait. I was only jesting." His footsteps were close behind her.

"If you *must* know," she said, a bit out of breath. "I was going to take the money and disappear to a new kingdom. I was going to become someone else. I was going to have a life of my own where decisions aren't made for me. Where I can be my own person."

He caught up to her as they exited the cave in the evening air. The sun was dipping close to the horizon now. Her heart thumped a wild beat as she peered at the sky. It was almost sunset. He paused next to her, likely thinking the same thing as he looked toward the west.

"It would be a terrible thing if you became someone else." His words were quiet.

Rosamund turned to look at him and noticed the torch in his hand was now unlit. He tossed it aside and took her hand in his. It was something he seemed to be doing a lot and, by the way he looked at her, enjoyed it.

In her other, she still held the coin.

"Would it be too terribly awful to marry me?" he asked.

There was heart rending tenderness in those honey-colored eyes of his, causing a tingling to erupt in the pit of her stomach. The evening sunlight illuminated the gold strands in his dark hair. There was a tangible bond between them. Whether it was because they were pushed together by happenstance or magic, she did not know. And, frankly, she didn't care anymore.

Finally, she shook her head. "No, it wouldn't."

He reached for her then, cupping her face in his hands and stepping closer. Her pulse beat at the base of her throat, as though her heart had moved from its usual place. Anticipation swelled through her as he leaned closer. Her eyes fluttered closed. Her lips parted, ready and willing and wanting.

A wicked laugh broke through their happy bubble. Her eyes flew open, meeting his only a moment before he stepped back, pushing her behind him, and wielding his sword. A woman stood several feet away. She was dressed in a black gown. Black feathers plumed from her shoulders, curving upward and swaying with her steps. She wore a black choker around her throat adorned with something that appeared to sparkle. She had long, slender fingers with black nails ending in deadly points. On her head, an onyx crown glittered like mirrored shafts of light.

"How delightful." Her dark red lips spread in a fiendish smile. "The two of you make such a lovely couple."

"Who are you? What do you want?" Phillip kept the sword pointed at the woman.

"Why, I want the princess. It is her birthday, after all."

A sudden coldness spread through her as she stared at the woman in front of them. She clutched her elbows. "You're the dark faery."

She clucked her tongue and looked wounded. "That is such an ugly phrase. I am Queen Rowena, ruler of the Eternal Court of Faery. And I have come to exact my revenge."

Rosamund tensed, every muscle going rigid. She glanced at the sky to see the sun dipping closer to the horizon.

If she recalled the curse properly, it was that she would prick her finger on a thorn before the sun set on her eighteenth birthday. There were no thorns here.

"You will stay away from her," Phillip said.

"How sweet you think you can protect her."

"It was you, wasn't it?" Rosamund asked. "You pushed us together. You sent us on this quest."

"How clever you are, dear girl. I take many forms. Olga, the old woman, for one. A dragonfly that talked, for another." There was a knowing glint in her eyes.

Rosamund gasped. "That was you in the garden! You urged me to run away."

"Stephan removed all the roses from the castle grounds. I had to do *something*."

"Why push us together?" Phillip demanded.

"Because I needed a witness."

With a wave of her hand, his sword flew from his grasp. It landed several feet away near the queen. Phillip whipped out his dagger, pointing it in her direction. Again, she used her magic to make it fly from his grasp. Defenseless, he pushed his body between Rosamund and the queen as if he were a human shield.

Rowena chanted something under her breath and in an instant, vines sprouted from the ground on either side of the cave opening. As they grew taller and taller, the lethal thorns grew from the stems followed by large, fragrant roses.

Phillip took her by the hand and darted to the left, but more roses grew. He turned to the right. Still more bushes. They were trapped between the roses. The only thing left to do was charge toward the queen who stood with her arms outstretched as she chanted her spell. He cut Rosamund glance. She gave him a go-ahead nod. Together, they bolted toward the queen.

In an instant, she transformed from the queen into a great black dragon. Phillip halted as Rosamund emitted a squeal of surprise. Rowena turned her giant head toward them, her red serpentine eyes piercing them both.

"There is no escape from the curse," the beast said.

Phillip spun around to her, gripping her by the shoulders. "Run, Rose!"

He gave her a shove away from him. But the scent of roses beckoned her. Fragrant and sweet, the blooms were large, with petals the size of her fist in pink, red, and white. The bushes towered over her, rocking toward her with the breath of the dragon.

"Rose!" he shouted.

The beast chuckled.

She stepped away from him. Her gaze transfixed on the large rosebush to her left. She was dimly aware Phillip tried to move toward her, to reach for her, but the dragon shoved her head between them and snarled a warning.

A voice flickered through her mind. The voice of the dragonfly from the garden. The one that told her to run away and never return. Now it told her to reach for the roses.

"Reach for it. Touch it," Rowena's voice urged.

Rosamund stretched out her hand toward the thorn.

"Rose, stop!"

"Enough," the dragon said on a growl.

She blew out a puff of smoke toward him, encasing him in a thick cloud. Phillip staggered away from the dragon, as though suddenly he was at a great distance. He watched in horror as the space expanded between them, gradually moving the princess farther and farther away from him.

Phillip tried to move toward Rosamund, to stop her from touching the thorn, but he was frozen in place. He felt light-headed. His vision blurred. His mind was foggy. He couldn't think clearly. He couldn't force his feet to move to keep her from touching that thorn.

The dragon's breath must be some type of magic to keep him in place so that he would have to watch as Rose staggered toward that thorny bush with her hand outstretched. Her other hand was still clutched into a tight fist.

Her name slipped from his lips in a plea. But she didn't hear him. She moved toward the rosebush, toward the one branch that appeared to be reaching back for her with giant pink blooms and thorns so large they looked menacing.

"Touch the thorn," Rowena urged.

He blinked, trying to clear his vision. In his haze, he saw the faery queen had morphed back into her true form and was no longer a dragon. She stood between him and Rosamund, her hands outstretched.

Phillip, in his haze, understood what was happening. Rosamund was under the same type of spell they were under the entire journey. She was compelled to reach for the thorn. Just as he was compelled to remain in place.

He tried to move again, but his limbs were heavy. As though he was trying to walk under water.

The sun dripped closer to the horizon. The day was almost over.

Rosamund, with her hand still outstretched, reached for the bush that shifted toward her, beckoning her closer. Even from his distance, he saw the deadly outline of sharp thorns.

"Touch the thorn, princess," Rowena urged in a dark and dangerous tone.

He tried to cry out, to warn Rosamund, but his voice was frozen in his throat.

Rosamund's hand moved closer. The tip of her forefinger touched the largest thorn on the bush. Shocked, she flushed hot as a bead of blood swelled where she pricked it. Her eyes fluttered closed and she tumbled to the ground. Her clutched fist opened and the gold coin rolled out.

The sleeping curse had taken hold of her.

Just as she fell, his eyelids turned to lead and he, too, fell to the ground. His legs were no longer able to hold him upright.

The last thing he heard was Rowena's distant, triumphant cackle. And then there was nothing at all.

CHAPTER 25

"Phillip! Wake up!"

The distant voice urged him to come back to life, but he felt as though he were incased in lead. It was hard to move his limbs and his eyes refused to open. Someone shook him and shouted his name in his ear again. He realized, dimly, it was Jeffrey trying to rouse him.

He peeled his eyes open and focused on Jeffrey's face hovering over him. Firelight flickered over his face creased with concern. He held a torch aloft to give them some light. With his free hand, his friend reached for him and helped to a sitting position. His head throbbed like mad as he tried to focus on his surroundings.

He was not surprised to see Jeffrey and Charles. His friend was an excellent tracker. He only wished they had arrived before sundown and Rosamund was compelled to prick her finger. Perhaps they would have had a better chance at fighting off the dark faery and her deadly Fae magic.

Charles kneeled next to the princess, the worry evident on his youthful face.

"

"I cannot rouse her," he said.

Phillip shook his head. "You won't be able to. It's the sleeping curse."

"There are no rosebushes here." Jeffrey glanced around in the deepening twilight.

Through his haze, Phillip took in their surroundings and realized that, indeed, there were no roses anymore. They must have disappeared along with Rowena when her curse had finally taken hold of Rosamund.

"There were," he said, his voice rough and raw. "The dark faery was here."

"Here? Was there treasure?" There was hint of excitement in Jeffrey's voice as he peered behind him into the darkened cave which was now nothing more than a black opening.

"No." Phillip climbed to his feet, his head objecting to the movement. "It was all a fiction."

Regret and disappointment shifted through him. Regret for falling for the dark faery's spell. Disappointment for not finding anything but one gold coin. He stepped toward Rosamund, falling to his knees by her sleeping form. The coin was in the dirt beside her. He picked up and tucked it in his pocket for safekeeping.

Charles rolled her to her back. She looked to be at peace as she slept. Her cheeks were flushed. The finger she pricked still had a dot of blood. He picked up her hand and held it in his as he peered down at her.

The guilt was almost insurmountable. He should have never led her here. They should have found way to fight the compulsion spell and take her back home where she would have been safe.

Then she would still be awake. Or would she? Would the dark faery find a way to make sure Rose fell under her curse anyway? He was certain she would have. She'd long harbored deep-seated vengeance.

"What do we do now?" Charles asked, his voice hollow and thin.

"How do we break the curse?" Jeffrey asked.

Phillip shook his head. "I don't know."

"You were there that day when she was cursed," Jeffrey said.

"I can't remember if the Fae queen said how to break it." And that frustrated him, too. "We should probably take her back to her father."

"Like this?" Jeffrey pointed to her sleeping form. "How do we explain that?"

"We tell the king and queen the truth," Phillip said. "I will make my apologies to them."

"It's not your fault," Charles said.

"It is," he insisted. "The moment I knew who she was, I should have insisted we return her home."

Jeffrey placed a hand on his shoulder in comfort. "The curse was unavoidable, I think. Even if you had returned her home, the dark faery would have found a way to make sure it happened."

His friend voiced his own thoughts about the curse and the dark faery. It gave him little comfort.

"There's a town nearby. I'll see if I can buy a wagon or cart," Jeffrey said.

Phillip gave him a quizzical look. "Why?"

"To transport the sleeping princess."

He nodded. Yes, of course, they would need some way to carry her back home. And then he would face the consequences for her sleeping curse. Whatever they may be.

Though he was initially aggravated by Jeffrey's and Charles's arrival, he was grateful now that his friend took charge to find a way to return with the princess. He wondered, too, if his parents were still there waiting for his eventual appearance. What, exactly, would they think when he arrived with Princess Rosamund in her sleeping curse?

Jeffrey handed Charles the torch. "Build a fire and set up camp. I will return as soon as I can."

Charles nodded to his brother as he rode away, leaving the two of them behind with the horses and the sleeping princess.

What was happening to her? Rosamund didn't understand.

One moment she was standing near the cave inhaling the sweet scent of roses for the first time, the next she was here in this dreadful place surrounded by shadow and darkness. A surge of panic gripped her chest, each breath coming in short gasps as she frantically searched for any semblance of familiarity in the unsettling environment that surrounded her. Where was she?

"Hello?"

Silence was her answer. She moved deeper into the shadows, but still saw or heard nothing. A growing fear pumped through her, making the skin on the back her neck tingle.

"Phillip? Where are you?"

She flung her arms through the shadows as if to swipe them away. The wispy clouds broke up for a moment, then reformed around her, keeping her in that dismal place.

How had she ended up here? She tried to think back to the last moment she recalled. She stood near the cave with Phillip. The coin was clutched in one hand. Phillip held the other. She looked around for the coin but it was nowhere to be found. Neither was Phillip.

Think, think! she admonished.

She was holding Phillip's hand and then he was about to kiss her. Yes! That was it. He cupped her face in his hands and all she thought was how warm his palms were against her chilled cheeks. And the scent of roses wafted over them, making it a beautiful, sweet, perfect moment. She was ready and willing and waiting for his lips to meet hers. Her heart did a funny thud in her chest and there was a curious sweeping of emotion in the pit of her stomach. Oh, how she wanted him to kiss her.

But then the dark faery arrived and interrupted. Phillip released her and shoved her behind him. He drew his sword. But the dark faery was having none of that. She swept his sword away with magic, then turned into a giant beast of a dragon.

All the while, Rosamund was enamored with the enormous roses with their soft petals dotted with dew and their aromatic scent drawing her closer and closer and closer.

Phillip shouted something to her. She wanted to turn to him, but couldn't. She wanted to cry out to him to help her, but couldn't. She wanted to stop herself from reaching out her hand, but couldn't.

Reach for it. Touch it.

But it was not the dark faery who spoke. It was the dragon. Her breath plumed around Rosamund in a misty fog, pushing her toward the branch with the wicked looking thorns. It swayed in the breeze toward her, reaching for her, beckoning her.

Rosamund gasped and pressed her fingertips against her lips.

"The curse. The thorn!" she whispered.

A sob escaped her as she clutched her elbows. The tip of her forefinger was sore. She glanced down at it to see a red dot where there appeared to be a prick from a thorn.

"No…" she whispered. "It can't be."

"I'm afraid it is."

The female voice startled her. She peered into the shadows look-ing for the person who spoke, but she saw nothing and no one. She clutched her elbows, her heart ramming hard in her chest.

"Who's there?"

The misty shadows swirled and a woman emerged. She was tall, beautiful, with a regal looking face and bright green eyes. She wore a velvet gown that matched her eyes. Her long red hair hung in waves over her shoulders as she approached. On her head she wore a silver circlet with intricate scrollwork that rested on her forehead.

"Hello, princess." Her deep red lips formed a smile.

"Who are you?" Rosamund resisted the urge to step away, but there was something calming and reassuring about the presence of someone else in her strange surroundings.

"I am Queen Elara of the Celestial Court."

Rosamund's eyes widened as she looked her over once more. She saw then, the delicate point of her ears. "You are from Faery."

She gave a slight nod of her head. "I am."

A strange sensation went over Rosamund as she peered at her, her skin prickling with gooseflesh. "Am I sleeping?"

"You are." She reached for her and took her hand in hers, turning her hand upward. She traced her forefinger, pausing at the sore spot. "By a thorn."

"That was the dark faery's curse, wasn't it?"

"I'm afraid it was," she agreed. She released her hand. Their eyes met. "Rowena is a vengeful faery. When she was left off the invitation list, she exacted her revenge on King Stephan and Queen Eleanor."

"Why would she curse me? I was an innocent child," Rosamund said.

"You were, indeed. But Rowena has a dark heart. Her court is the Eternal Court in the far reaches of Faery and she often feels as though she is not part of the Faery Realm. Not receiving an invitation to your christening was the final breaking point for her," Queen Elara said. "Rowena's curse was to have you prick your finger and die."

Panic bubbled through her. "She...wanted to kill me? Phillip said it was a sleeping curse. Am I dead?"

"No, child!" she said quickly. "Rowena wanted to make an example of you. To show her might and her power to us, the other Fae royals. However..." A small smile tugged at her lips and delight twinkled in her eyes. "I outwitted her. My Fae gift to you, princess, was that you would *not* die, but instead fall into a slumber."

Rosamund stared at her a long moment, trying to calm her racing heart. She was thankful she wasn't dead. Something, though, occurred to her.

"Rowena doesn't know you changed the curse, does she? She thinks I'm dead."

"It is conceivable she thinks that, yes."

Rosamund wasn't sure if that was good news or not. If the dark faery thought she was dead, then perchance Rowena would leave her and her family alone for the rest of their days. But there was still the issue of her in a deep slumber.

She thought of her father, then. If he hadn't invited the Fae royals to her christening, then she would never have been cursed. She huffed her displeasure.

"Why did my father invite the Fae royals anyway?"

"Because he fears us," she said. "He fears we want to expand our borders. He fears we will invade and take away his land. That is why he betrothed you to the prince in the north."

And Phillip's father, King Reginald, agreed to the match. Rosamund understood, then. But why keep their betrothal a secret? That was something Queen Elara could not explain.

The queen reached for her again, taking her hands and holding them tight. "But there is nothing to fear. Please tell King Stephan that is not the case. Faery does not wish to conquer Stonebridge lands."

"How can I tell him when I'm under a sleeping curse?"

"Dear child, the curse can be broken," she said.

"How?" Rosamund asked.

"With true love's kiss." She squeezed her hands one last time before releasing them.

Immediately, Rosamund thought of Phillip. But did she love him? And did he love her in return? Certainly, she had felt something for him over the last few days as they traveled together. Was it something more than the spell they were under? Was it real? She wanted it to be real. She *longed* for it to be real, for after traveling with Phillip and getting to know him, it was difficult to deny the affection she felt for him. Her heart thumped a wild beat thinking about it.

"But I...how do I..." She paced the small area of shadows.

"You must tell him," she urged.

Rosamund spun to face her. "How can I tell him?"

A knowing smile crossed her face. "You are a resourceful girl. You'll find a way."

"But—"

"Farwell, princess."

And then the queen was gone.

True to his word, Jeffrey returned with a cart in which to transport the princess. He arrived late into the night while Phillip was still awake keeping watch. Charles was fast asleep, curled in his bedroll near the fire.

Phillip used his own bedroll and hers to make sure she would be comfortable. Then he and Jeffrey lifted her into the cart. Phillip carefully tucked a blanket around her. When they were finished, he peered down at her still awash in his guilt.

"There was nothing you could have done," Jeffrey said, his voice quiet.

"I know that. But perhaps I should have tried harder."

"Tried harder to defeat the dark faery? You said yourself when she was in dragon form and she blew her breath at you, it paralyzed you," Jeffrey reminded him. He placed a hand on his shoulder and gave him a gentle pat. "Do you know how to break the curse?"

He shook his head. "I've been trying to remember the exact words of the curse when the dark faery placed it on her. But that was a long time ago and I was a child."

Frustration edged through him. He was trying to recall the words of the curse. All he remembered was that she would prick her finger and fall asleep. He recalled it was the second Fae queen who changed Rowena's curse from death to slumber. But was there something more? Was there a way to break the curse?

"It'll come to you." Jeffrey sounded so sure of it he almost believed him. "We should get some sleep."

"You go ahead. I'll keep watch," Phillip said.

His friend was about to object when he merely nodded and made his way toward the circle of firelight. He settled down in his bedroll next to his brother. Phillip couldn't sleep anyway so he stayed awake to keep an eye on the princess.

Not that he thought the dark faery would return. The damage was already done. He told himself it was because it was the right thing to do. That it had nothing to do with his feelings for her. He refused to believe there was anything more than friendship between them.

Though the way she looked at him sometimes made him think otherwise. The way she allowed him to take her by the hand. She never pulled away.

He wasn't sure what came over him when he cupped her face in his hands. A sudden urge to kiss her tugged at him. Her heart-shaped red lips beckoned. He would have kissed her, too, if Rowena hadn't interrupted.

Now, he was faced with an impossible task. Telling her parents she had pricked her finger on a thorn and fallen under the curse. He was not looking forward to that.

Phillip was still awake as the sun broke the horizon. As it rose, he moved to the cart where Rosamund—his Rose—slumbered on. As the sun emerged, the first rays fell upon her face, lighting it in a golden glow. For a moment, he thought her skin shimmered. He moved closer. Pale pink color was high in her round cheeks. Her lashes were long and dark. Her lips red as the rose. Strands of her hair golden hair sparkled in the dawn. As he peered closer, the sparkles of what could only be faery dust glistened on her cheeks.

Touched by Fae magic.

She'd said Charles told her that. He wasn't wrong. She truly was touched by Fae magic.

When he left Haven Castle, he was determined to forge his own way. He wanted nothing more than to be his own person, to forsake the betrothal to the princess.

And now...now his feelings had changed. Gazing at her, his heart lurched. He found himself eternally grateful the faery queen had altered the curse to keep her alive. He reached a hand toward her face, lightly brushing her cheek with his fingertips. Her skin continued to sparkle in the golden light of morning.

"Have you been awake all night?"

Jeffrey's voice startled him out of his thoughts. He turned to see his friend rolling up his bedroll.

"Yes. I couldn't sleep," he said.

Jeffrey nudged Charles awake. As his brother yawned and stretched, Jeffrey ordered him to break down camp while he made the horses ready.

"It's going to be a long day of hard riding," Jeffrey warned. "I hope you're ready for that."

Phillip inhaled a breath to quell his ratting nerves, then expelled it. "Ready as I'll ever be."

They broke camp and soon were on their way to Myst Hall where he would, at last, face his destiny.

CHAPTER 26

I t was early morning when they arrived at Myst Hall after nearly two days of hard riding, little food, and almost no sleep. Exhaustion hit Phillip hard as they rode up the dirt road to the castle with the sleeping princess in the cart in tow. His gut clenched into a tight knot as he faced the castle. He hadn't seen it since he was six years old.

He didn't know what to expect.

Someone must have sounded the alarm that there were visitors arriving for he saw several people exiting the castle. As they neared, he made out his parents as well as King Stephan and Queen Eleanor. His nerves were on high alert as dread coiled tight in his chest, making it ache.

Phillip came to a halt and dismounted from the horse pulling the cart. He inhaled a deep breath to calm his rattling nerves as he approached the four waiting royals, all with expectant looks on their faces. All but Queen Eleanor whose face was pinched with worry and fear.

Halting in front of them all, he bowed low to first his parents then Rosamund's.

"Your majesties," he greeted as he rose to his full height.

Stephan's gaze scanned the other riders and paused on the two riderless horses—one Phillip's and one Rosamund's.

"Where is my daughter?" he asked.

Swallowing hard, Phillip gestured toward the cart. Both the king and queen hurried over. As soon as they peered inside, the queen cried out, a sob choking her throat. The king stood at the side of the cart looking down at his sleeping daughter, his face devoid of color.

"What happened to her?"

"It was the sleeping curse—" Phillip began.

"I know it was the sleeping curse," Stephan snapped.

He turned his glowering gaze on him. The queen openly wept. Phillip's mother, Queen Adele, hurried to her side to comfort her by placing an arm around her shoulders. She whispered in her ear, trying to calm her.

"I spent nearly eighteen years making sure no rose or thorn would harm my daughter and yet here she sleeps." Stephan pointed to the cart. "I mean to know how this happened. Where has she been? With *you* all this time?"

Phillip shifted from one foot to the other, his hand clenched into a tight fist as he tried to decide how to answer. While true she hadn't been with him since the moment she escaped Myst Hall, it was also true she had traveled with him for the last several days.

"Well? The truth, boy!"

"King Stephan, enough of this." Reginald, his father, stepped up next to him. His large presence was a reassuring buffer between him and Rosamund's enraged father.

Phillip noticed Jeffrey and Charles had both dismounted and stood by their horses waiting to see how things were going to play out. Both remained mute, their faces devoid of emotion.

"It's clear they have been riding for days to reach us," Reginald said. "Give the boy a moment to collect his thoughts and tell us the story."

There was no mistaking the fury on Stephan's face as he glared at Phillip. His father gave him a nudge of encouragement.

"I met Rosamund in the Mystwood Forest," Phillip began. "She traveled alone. I feared for her safety, so I invited her to journey with me. I had no idea of her true identity at first. I thought she was merely a peasant girl lost in the woods.

"It was the dark faery who compelled us by a sinister spell she cast on both of us. She pushed us together and toward a cave where there were enormous rosebushes with thorns. I tried to stop her from touching the thorn." He paused as he looked at the cart where Rosamund slumbered. "But the power of the spell was too great."

Silence descended between them. The only sound that of the weeping queen. Phillip looked at his mother whose face was creased with her own sorrow.

"Forgive me, your majesty," Phillip said.

Stephan looked down at his daughter. He brushed her cheek with the back of his hand.

"She will be taken to her chamber. We will find a way to break the curse, even if I have to send for the Queen of the Celestial Court herself to tell me how," he said.

Phillip moved toward the cart but Stephan held up a hand to stop him. He halted mid-step.

"No. You will go with your parents to your own chambers. You will stay away from my daughter. I will allow you rest after your journey. However, in the morn, I expect the three of you to be gone from Myst Hall and never return."

"Stephan!" Eleanor said on a breath, surprise evident in her tone. "The betrothal—"

"We will not discuss it here or now," he snapped. Then his gaze cut to Phillip and Reginald. "The betrothal is hereby broken. There will be no wedding."

Phillip stared at the king then peered at the cart where she slumbered. His gut clenched into a tight knot. It was difficult for him to grasp their betrothal was broken just like that.

He glanced at his father to see his jaw was clenched, a muscle ticking along the edge. Though he tried to hide his ire, it was clear he was furious with the turn of events.

"If that is your decision, Stephan, so be it. We will pack our belongings and depart at dawn." He motioned for his wife to join them.

Reluctantly, Adele left Eleanor's side and joined the two of them. No more words were exchanged as they all headed inside the castle. Phillip stole a glance over his shoulder to see Jeffrey and Charles still standing by their horses. No doubt the two of them wondering what they should do next. Return to Haven Castle or remain until morning and depart with them. Phillip had nothing to offer them. He dared not speak with King Stephan for he didn't wish to tempt his wrath further.

Exhaustion pounded through him as he followed his parents through the halls of the castle and up the stairs where they entered a large bedchamber that was big enough for the three of them. The living area hosted a chaise near the large fireplace. On the other side of the chaise, two oversized chairs with a small table between them. The floor was covered in a garnet plush rug. Several candelabras were lit in the room, giving it a warm inviting glow.

Phillip made for the chaise near the fireplace and immediately collapsed onto it. He was bone weary from all the traveling and near faint from not having eaten a full meal in days. As soon as the door was closed, sealing them inside the chamber away from prying eyes and listening ears, his father spoke.

"We should leave at once. I don't think we wait until morning."

"Nonsense," his mother said. "Can't you see Phillip is exhausted? And what of Jeffrey and Charles? Someone should see to it they can stay here tonight. Furthermore, I don't think we should leave so soon."

Phillip cracked open an eye to see his mother standing with her hands on her hips in defiance of his father, whose face was crimson with ire.

"Why should we stay? Stephan called off the wedding and broke faith with us."

"Stephan is grieving for his daughter and so is Eleanor," Adele said. "He made an emotional decision. We must think this through with a cool head, my love. Just because he wants us to leave by the morning doesn't mean we should."

"Have you gone mad, my wife? We cannot stay here."

"Shush, Reginald." Then she bustled over to Phillip with a swish of her skirts. She lowered herself to the ground, the material of her gown billowing out around her as she reached for him. "My dear, there has to be more to the story than what you told us."

Phillip shook his head from side to side. "There isn't, Mother."

"Poppycock." She stood straight, her fists once again on her hips. "I'm going to ring for tea and refreshments and then you're going to tell us *exactly* what happened."

"Mother—"

"I won't hear any objections from either you *or* your father. Understood?"

"Adele—"

"I mean that," she said cutting off his father.

If he hadn't been so weary, he would have laughed. When his mother made up her mind to do something, there was no stopping her. She was like a battering ram and stronger willed than him or his father. Sheer determination sparkled in her eyes. He knew that look and saw it many times as a boy.

Though what she intended to do with the truth once she had it, he didn't know.

It seemed both he and Rosamund got their wish—their wedding was called off. So, why, then did he have the stinging sensation of disappointment?

His mother was a patient woman. She waited while he stuffed himself with a late breakfast. His father had long retired to their bed chamber to nap or brood. She poured a cup of tea for herself, one for him, and then sat in the chair by the cold fireplace. She held the cup and saucer, giving him a pointed look over the top of it.

"Well?"

He heaved a sigh. "Where shall I begin, Mother?"

"At the beginning. How and where did you meet the princess?"

Reaching for his cup of tea, he took a sip of the strong brew. He wished it was something stronger. He wished he were anywhere else but here under the piercing gaze of his mother.

He began his story with the night he slipped out of the castle with a packed bag. Jeffrey had promised to escort him to meet the princess the following morning and he was going to do all within his power to avoid the girl and the marriage.

It took all night and the next day to reach the Mystwood Forest. When night had fallen, he searched for shelter and happened upon the cottage in the woods. Much to his surprise, someone else was already there.

"It was the princess," he said. "At the time, I didn't know who she was. She merely told me her name was Rose. She shared her bread with me. There was a loft where she slept that night while I took the floor beside the fire."

He smiled, recalling how she had doted on him and made sure he was comfortable before darting back up the stairs. The way she gathered the cushions and created a makeshift bed for him endeared her to him.

"She didn't know who you were, either, I gather," his mother said.

"No. I gave her a false name. I assumed she was a peasant girl and if she knew I was a prince, then perhaps she would not treat me the same."

"The same?" she asked.

"We were able to behave as ourselves without the stuffiness of court politics or formalities."

His mother took a sip of her tea, hiding a knowing smile behind her cup. Though she tried to hide it, he saw. He knew she was forming her own assessment of the situation and making assumptions. It was exactly why he did not want to tell her the truth.

"Go on," she urged.

He picked up the tale with their breakfast in the tavern and how Myst Hall soldiers questioned them. How he had lied to them because her face had paled when she saw them. He was aware they were after her yet something inside him kept him from handing her over to them. If he had, things would have ended right there.

"That was when I realized she was no more a peasant than me. She told me she was the Princess of Myst and that she refused to return home." He lifted his gaze from his tea and looked at his mother. "Because she did not want to marry."

"It seems you both had that in common, then."

Nodding, he said, "I should have told her right then who I was."

"But you didn't."

"No."

"Why?"

One shoulder lifted in a shrug. "I feared what she would do when she found out."

"But she did find out?" she asked.

"She did."

It was then he told her about the old hag in the cabin, the map to the treasure, how Jeffrey and Charles found them on the road and Jeffrey addressed him as prince. How angry Rosamund was when she discovered the truth about him.

"It was then I knew we should all go to Myst Hall. That we should return the princess home," he said.

"Why didn't you?" The queen was genuinely interested in his answer.

"It is difficult to explain." He took a sip of tea, stalling.

She waited, patiently, as she refilled her cup and dropped in one cube of sugar, stirred, and then sipped. Her expectant gaze was still on him.

"It was as though there was some driving force pushing us together onward. Deeper into the forest. We both felt it and we were both powerless to resist."

He finished telling her the rest of the story about the dragon's cave, the treasure that wasn't there and, finally, the appearance of Queen Rowena. She used her dark magic to conjure the rosebushes and force Rosamund to prick her finger. When he fell silent, he sipped his tea and leaned back in the chair, the exhaustion pounding through him.

His mother had a funny look on her face. One he had seen numerous times as she inspected him with a sort of tranquil calm. He had the distinct feeling her mind was at work with some scheming plan or thought.

"What, Mother?"

She was silent a long moment, then very carefully placed the tea cup on the table in front of her. She sat back in the chair, her hands flat in her lap.

"You're in love with the princess."

Phillip was so stunned by her declaration, he sat straight in the chair, his hands on his knees as he leaned toward her.

"I never said that."

"No, but you are." She gave him a knowing smile.

He huffed out a breath. "You don't know that. You can't know that."

And yet, when he thought of Rosamund, a warmth spread through him. There was something about her that he found attractive and sweet. When she looked at him and gave him her smile, his heart swelled. There was a light of life and vitality within her lovely emerald eyes. She was brave, and kind, and charming, and—

Bollocks.

He was in love with her.

"Phillip, my darling, you've spent a good portion of your youth chasing women who amused you. When you had your fill of them, you discarded them. You broke their hearts. But Rosamund is different. She is more than a passing fancy. You'll never admit it, though you should. Perhaps you don't want to admit it because you were betrothed and forced into a marriage neither of you wanted. And here you are, pining away for her while she is in an eternal slumber."

Much as he didn't want to admit it, his mother was right. He rubbed his forehead, trying to will away the sudden headache that had taken up residence there.

"What is your point, Mother?"

"My point is you need to find a way to break the curse and see if she feels the same way about you."

He dropped his hand to look at her and saw a profound re-solve shining brightly in her eyes. His heart raced as he sat a little straighter and scooted to the edge of the cushion to lean toward his mother.

"Whatever you're scheming, you can stop it," he said.

A brow lifted. "Scheming? My dear, if the princess loves you and you love her, then I see no reason to call off the wedding." Suddenly, she jumped to her feet. "I must speak with Queen Eleanor at once."

With her skirts bustling, she hurried to the door.

He knew exactly where she was going. With a groan, he leaned back into the chair once again.

CHAPTER 27

R osamund was trapped within the land of shadows and darkness. When Queen Elara left her, she had no other visitors. Madness was beginning to set in as she paced.

She was grateful the queen told her how to break the curse. However, that didn't seem to help her much since she was stuck within the small confines of her inner prison. The queen told her she was resourceful, but she had yet to figure out *how* to break free of her mental jail and contact Phillip.

Thinking of him made her pause her pacing. She clutched her elbows, remembering the way his warm hands cupped her face. The way his breath shuddered out between his lips that sweet moment before he intended to kiss her. He's honey colored eyes were half-lidded. It was the last thing she remembered before closing hers, because she had decided to memorize everything about that moment.

That was before everything went wrong. Before Rowena arrived. Before she blew her dragon's breath on each of them to control them and force them to do her bidding.

"Oh, Phillip. How can I reach you?"

Her voice came out a whisper as she spoke to no one. There was no one to hear her plea. No one to help her claw her way out of her forced confinement.

"I must find a way," she told herself.

But how?

She thought of Phillip again. His strong jaw. The way he smiled when he looked at her and made her insides warm. The way her stomach fluttered when he took her by the hand. She was happy to be with him, to ride alongside him. Their grand adventure turned out to be nothing more than a ridiculous sham, but it was still a grand adventure.

Every moment they spent together was another moment she cherished. She had never wanted it to end. When he asked her if it was terribly awful to marry him, she immediately knew her answer. No, it would not be terribly awful to marry him. Suddenly, she found she *wanted* to marry him and would happily do so when they returned.

"Oh, dear me," she said on a breath. She pressed her cold, shaking fingers to her lips as she stared into the nothingness before her. "I'm in love with Phillip."

The realization slammed into her so hard, her heart ached. There was an immediate throbbing at the base of her skull. As the breath whooshed out of her, she collapsed to the ground, drawing up her knees and encircling them with her arms.

"Phillip, I love you," she whispered to no one. "All you have to do is kiss me and the curse will be broken."

Would it? Must he love her in return for it to work? She didn't know. She didn't know if he loved her in return. She didn't know if his kiss would break the curse.

She had to find a way. She just had to!

She rested her chin on her knees. Her eyes were heavy with fatigue as she sat there rocking back and forth trying to remain awake. To think. She had to think of a way to get to Phillip, to wake up so she could then tell her father the Fae were not interested in Stonebridge.

The queen's words came back to her. *You are a resourceful girl. You'll find a way.*

She focused on one thing—Phillip.

Her mind drifted. Then she thought for sure she saw him. She shot to her feet as she peered at him, slumped in a chair. He was sleeping with his head leaned against the back of the cushion. Something startled him and he awoke. Those honey-colored eyes of his met hers. Her heart leapt as she gasped.

"Rose?"

"I'm here!"

She wanted to rush to him, but the gloom was between them. Try as she might, she could not push it aside and go to him.

"Where is here?" Confusion was written all over his handsome face.

"I'm stuck in this place of darkness and shadows."

He rose to his full height and tried to take a step toward her, but he was unable. That same murkiness kept him from coming closer. "How is this possible? I was in the castle and fell asleep and now I'm here with you."

She understood then. The realization hit her like a bolt of lightning. She was in his dream. Perhaps thinking of him had placed her there while he was relaxed.

"You're dreaming," she said. "I'm in your dream!"

"How do I find you?"

She ignored his question and rushed on. "It's the sleeping curse. You have to break it."

He spread his hands as if in surrender. "I don't know how."

"I do. You must find me, Phillip."

"Your father...he said he was taking you to your bedchamber."

He was starting to fade from her. Somewhere in the distance, she heard another voice. A man. It sounded as though it were Jeffrey. He must be trying to wake Phillip. Panic swept through her.

"Go there! Go to my bedchamber at once."

A dense dark fog rolled in between them. She was only able to make out a silhouette of him and nothing more. His face faded from her sight.

"No, not yet," she said, her voice a roughened whispered. "Not yet."

"Then what? Rose! Where are you? I can't see you anymore."

More shadows as the gloom pressed in between them, blotting him out. She blurted out the only words that came to mind.

"True love's kiss!"

And then he was gone. Her shoulders slumped as she collapsed to the ground. Hot tears stung her eyes. She had no idea if her message got through to him. She hoped it had.

Phillip awoke with a start to see Jeffrey standing over him, a worried look on his face.

"Are you all right, mate? You were thrashing in your sleep."

"Jeffrey? How did you get here?"

"Your mother brought me and Charles here," he said.

But he really didn't hear his answer as the dream crashed into him with a fury. He shoved Jeffrey out his way as he shot to his feet. He raked his hand through his hair, his heart beating at a rapid pace.

She'd told him to go to her bedchamber at once. The last thing he recalled before the dream faded was her voice shouting *true love's kiss.*

Had he heard that right? She wanted him to kiss her to break the curse? There was only one way to find out.

"I need to find Rose."

"I don't think her father will allow you to see her," Jeffrey said.

He spied Charles lounging in the chair opposite him, his ankle propped on his knee as he munched on a lemon cake.

"The king was fairly unhappy with you," Charles pointed out.

"I don't care about that," Phillip snapped, impatience lancing through him. He turned to Jeffrey, grasped him by the upper arms and squeezed. "I know how to break the curse."

His friend blinked surprise as his face went devoid of all emotion. "You do?"

"Yes! I have to get to her. I have to find her."

He shoved him away and darted for the door.

"Wait, Phillip." Jeffrey hurried after him and grabbed his arm to pull him to a stop. "You can just go charging through the castle."

He focused on his friend, his mind still racing with thoughts of Rose. His Rose. "Why not?"

"Because the king has posted guards outside your door," he said. "That's why."

"That does pose a problem," Charles said from his chair.

Before Phillip was able to reply, his mother burst through the door of their chambers. Her face was flushed as though she'd made a mad dash through the hallways. Before she closed the door behind her, he got a glimpse of the two guards standing on either side of the door. Jeffrey was right.

"Phillip!" She said his name on a breath.

"Where have you been, Mother?"

"I've just come from speaking with the queen. I told her what you told me about—"

"Mother!" he admonished.

But she pressed on without pausing. "She does not want to call off the wedding. But we *must* find a way for you to break the curse—"

"I know how, Mother."

She clamped her mouth closed and drew up straight, blinking surprise. "You do?"

"Yes, and I need to get to Rose *now*."

Calm passed over her features. Then she gave one quick nod and held her hand out to him.

"Come with me, dear. I'll take you to her."

CHAPTER 28

When the door closed behind them, both guards gave them a sideways look. His mother dipped a quick curtsy and gave them her best congenial smile.

"I'm taking my son to the gardens for a late afternoon walk. I hope that's all right?"

The guard on the left nodded. "Very well. But only the gardens."

"Of course!"

She gripped his hand tight in one hand and in the other her skirt as she hurried down the hallway out of sight from the guards. She headed for the staircase.

"How do you know where her chamber is?" he asked, a bit out of breath.

"That's where I met Queen Eleanor." Though she walked at a brisk pace, she did not sound out of breath.

His mother amazed him. He had no idea how she managed to get an audience with the queen while in the princess's bedchamber, but he was grateful. She released his hand and picked up her skirts, holding them with both hands as she practically sprinted down the stone steps. He followed closely behind her and came to a jarring halt when he realized she'd stopped at the foot of the staircase.

"Wait here one moment," she said on a breathy whisper.

She hurried around a corner, her footsteps so light she made not a sound. Then she returned a moment later and grasped him by the hand again, tugging him along behind her without a word. He said nothing as he followed her through the corridors, the great hall, and then to another set of stairs. She released his hand, picked up her skirts, and ascended quickly.

"The royal family's chambers are here in the north tower," she said as she climbed the stairs. "I'll take you straight to Rosamund's chamber."

"Thank you, Mother," he said, panting.

His legs burned hot with his quick ascension, his heart beating so fast he thought it might pound right out of his chest. Not to mention the explosion of sudden nerves that skittered through him at the thought kissing her and trying to break the curse.

True Love's Kiss!

Her words rang in his head as they paused at a door. His mother gave a swift knock and then stepped behind him. There was such a long bit of silence, he thought for sure no one was coming to the door. He lifted his hand about to knock again when the door opened and he came face to face with Queen Eleanor. Surprise flickered over her features as their gazes met.

He bowed low. "Your majesty."

"What are you doing here? If Stephan finds you here—"

"I brought him," his mother said from behind him. "He knows how to break the curse."

The queen's eyes went wide and round as she stepped aside and ushered him into the chamber.

"This way," she said.

She didn't even wait to close the door behind him. A quick glance over his shoulder to see his mother stepping inside to do just that. Then she stood in front of the door as though a sentry.

Phillip followed the queen through the palatial suite, not taking time to really look at his surroundings. He had one thing on his mind—get to the princess. At the bedchamber, the queen halted and made a motion for him to go inside.

The door was open. Inside the suite, he saw the oversized four-poster bed draped in gossamer curtains as if to hide the sleeping figure on the feather mattress. He hesitated, his heart throbbing. The queen placed a reassuring hand on his shoulder.

"Prince Phillip?"

He turned to look at her and saw the question and concern etched on her face. "How will you break the curse?"

His mouth had gone dry and yet he swallowed hard. "With a kiss."

She said nothing, merely gave a nod and stepped back away from the door. Looking at the princess, he steeled his nerves. His hands were clenched into tight fists as he approached the bed. Rosamund laid on her back, her hands folded on her chest. Her face was in repose, making her look calm and serene.

He pushed aside the curtain and perched on the side of the bed beside her. She looked so beautiful there he couldn't resist brushing her cheek with the back of his hand. Her silken skin was cool to the touch. And it still shimmered.

Kissed by Fae magic.

He leaned down and closed his eyes. His lips met hers in a gentle, sweet kiss that held all his hope, his faith, his love that she would wake. Despite her sleeping form, her lips were warm and soft. He straightened and waited, holding his breath. Nothing happened for a long, silent moment.

And then her eyes opened. Her gaze met his. His heart tripped in his chest as a small smile pulled up the corners of her mouth.

Phillip blew out the breath he was holding.

He reached for her, cupping her face in one of his hands. "Rose. My springtime Rose."

"You did it," she said, her voice tinged with wonder and admiration. "You heard me?"

"I heard you in my dream. True love's kiss."

Color rose high in her cheeks as she flushed. He was certain he saw the pounding of her pulse in the long column of her neck. Rosamund came to a sitting position and, in one forward motion, wrapped her arms around his neck. It caught him so off guard, he didn't immediately react. She buried her face against his throat, her warm cheek pressed against his skin. He wrapped his arms around her in a tight embrace and held her.

Rosamund pulled away a bit, tipped her head back and gazed up at him with such adoration in her big emerald eyes, his heart thudded hard against his ribcage. In that instant, something intense flared between them. He understood everything he felt for her was real. The magic spell may have brought them together, but it was not an enchantment that made him fall in love with her. It was her that made him fall in love with her. Everything about her.

Her gaze traveled over his face and searched his eyes and then she did the most unexpected thing of all. She pulled him to her, pressing her lips against his in a caress that left him breathless and lightheaded. A kiss that was as tender and light as the springtime breeze.

In the bliss of that moment, he thought he heard the quiet gasp of the queen.

It was enough to snap her back to her senses. She pulled away, her lips damp and pink in the aftermath of their kiss. A breath shuddered out between her lips.

She pressed her forehead against his and dropped her voice so low only he heard. "I love you, Phillip."

Though the curse broke with his kiss, it was still nice to hear her say the words. To confirm her feelings for him. His heart squeezed as he realized the impossibility that his own feelings for her were real.

"I love you, Rose."

She turned her head to see her mother hovering in the doorway of her bedchamber, tears in her eyes and her cheeks pink with color. Confusion creased her face.

"I'm home?"

"Yes," he said, still holding her. He was reluctant to release her. She was warm and soft against him and he found he quite liked having her near him.

"How?"

"Jeffrey found a cart. The three of us brought you home. Rose, I should tell you...your father was rather distressed when he saw you had succumbed to the sleeping curse."

She sucked in a sharp breath. "My father. I must tell him."

Rosamund pushed out of his arms and scrambled off the bed. She wobbled on her feet and placed a hand on the side of her head as if the quick movement was too much for her. He leapt up to catch her and steadied her. She flashed a grateful smile.

"Must tell him what?" he asked.

"That the Fae are not interested in Stonebridge," she said.

"How do you know that?"

She started to reply, but her mother bustled into the bedchamber, her arms outstretched. When Rosamund saw her, she released Phillip and went to her. They hugged, her mother sniffing with her tears of joy. Then she pulled back, holding the princess at arm's length.

"I'm so relieved the curse is broken. And so will your father," the queen said.

"Mother, I need to speak with Papa at once," she said.

"Oh…" She sucked in a breath as she glanced from the princess to Phillip. He saw the apprehension in her eyes. "He's resting now, dear. I'll ring for tea and we can discuss—"

"Now, Mother," Rosamund said, her tone firm.

She blinked surprise. "But—"

"It's important. It's about the Fae."

Her mother drew her lower lip through her teeth and then nodded. "If it's that important."

"It is."

The queen cut him a glance. "Under the circumstances, Prince Phillip, I think you should return to your chambers with your mother."

He nodded. "Yes, of course."

"Why? What's happened?" Rosamund demanded.

"I will explain." Queen Eleanor took her by the hand and led her away.

As they exited the chamber, he had a terrible feeling he wouldn't see her again. He hoped he was wrong.

CHAPTER 29

Rosamund didn't understand what the circumstances were her mother spoke of as she followed her out of the bedchamber. She stole a glance over her shoulder to see Phillip's crestfallen face and worried something terrible had transpired when she was under the curse.

What had happened?

Her mother opened the door to the chamber to exit into the hallway. When she did, Queen Adele was waiting on the other side. She paced the length of the hallway, her skirts swishing with the movement. When she saw them, she came to a jarring halt. Her face lit with joy when she saw Rosamund. She rushed over to them.

"Princess!"

Without waiting for her to respond, she swept Rosamund into a great hug, holding her in a tight embrace that nearly squeezed the life out of her. For a moment, she was too stunned by the sudden action to react. When it was clear Queen Adele was not going to release her, she wrapped her arms around her and returned the hug. The queen smelled like lilacs.

At last, the queen pulled back and looked her over. Her broad smile was infectious and Rosamund found she was unable to resist returning the smile.

"My son was successful in breaking the curse, I see. How wonderful!"

"Your majesty," she said and tried to dip a curtsy.

"None of that," Adele said. "We are to be family soon." Her gaze flickered to her mother who remained behind her.

Queen Eleanor cleared her throat. "Yes, well, that remains to be seen."

Alarm suddenly pounded through Rosamund. "What do you mean, Mother?"

Her lips thinned into a straight line. She held her hand out to her. "Come. I will tell you as we walk." Then her gaze landed on Queen Adele. "I will let you know the outcome of the discussion I have with my husband."

"Good luck and godspeed," Queen Adele said.

Something wasn't right. Rosamund took her mother's hand and they began walking toward her parent's private chamber. Her heart pounded in her throat as they walked.

"Mother, what's happened?"

"Dearest, you know your father has a bit of a temper when he's pushed to his limits. After you disappeared and we had no idea where you were…" She paused, took a deep breath. "Well, he was beside himself with worry. We both were."

Guilt pounded through her for putting her parents through that. "I'm sorry, Mother. I shouldn't have left. But I was just so angry about the betrothal. A dragonfly came to me in the gardens and urged me to run away."

"A dragonfly?" She halted and turned to her, confusion written on her face.

Realizing what she said, Rosamund flushed. Now she would have to explain. "Yes, well, you see...the dark faery takes many forms. One of them was a dragonfly. She urged me to leave the castle. I shouldn't have listened but there was something that pushed me into it. It's difficult to explain."

She glanced down at their clasped hands, the shame of her past actions burning through her.

Her mother placed her hand under her chin and gently lifted her face up. Their eyes met. She gave her a soft smile.

"I understand. Queen Adele came to me. She told me the tale of how you and Phillip met and how the curse came to be. The dark faery, this Queen Rowena, was determined to make sure you pricked your finger on the thorn. Despite everything we did to keep you safe." She paused then, contemplation coming over her features. "I daresay no matter what we did would have kept you safe from this vengeful faery."

"I believe you're right, Mother."

They resumed walking.

"When Phillip arrived with you under the curse, you father was furious. He broke the betrothal and told King Reginald to return home at once."

Her gut clenched in fear. She reached for her mother, placing a hand on her arm. "But you talked him out of that, right?"

Her mother's expression was the only answer she needed. She gave a slow shake of her head.

"I see…" Rosamund said and glanced down the hallway at the closed door of her parent's chamber.

"But Queen Adele came to me and told me everything that happened between you and Phillip. And just now, when he broke the curse…" Her words trailed off.

Rosamund looked at her mother. "I love him."

Her face softened. She gave her a weak smile. "I know, dearest. That is why we must not let the wedding be canceled." She gripped her hands, squeezing them. "You have to tell him the truth."

Fear skipped through her. She was never good at talking with her father. She much preferred talking with her mother, who was often a buffer between the two of them.

"Can you do that?" she asked.

Rosamund nodded. "Yes."

"Good."

Another quick squeeze of her hands and then she released her and resumed walking again. In the short walk to the door, Rosamund thought about what she would say to her father, how she would say it. She knew her father had quite the temper and so she feared he would never listen to her or take her word as the truth.

Her mother didn't bother to knock on the door before she pushed it open. She led her inside, pausing to close it behind her.

"Wait here. I will speak to him first."

Rosamund nodded as she paused there in the main living chamber of the royal private quarters while her mother bustled to her father's private sitting area. The swish of her skirts was the only sound.

Rosamund shifted from one foot to the other. She realized then she was still dressed as the commoner in the clothes Anne gave her. Her boots were muddy and covered in dirt. Her pants were soiled. Her sleeves tattered from when the goblin attacked her. Her hands had scratches along the palms from that attack. Her forefinger was still sore from where she pricked it on the thorn.

She wondered, idly, where the gold coin had gone that Phillip gave her from the dragon's cave. The last thing she recalled was having it clenched in her fist.

As these thoughts passed through her mind, her father ran from his private sitting chamber and came to a halt several feet from her, his face ashen as though he might have seen a ghost. As though he didn't quite believe her mother when she told him the curse was broken.

"My darling girl." His voice was but a whisper. Her mother appeared at his side and gave him a nudge.

He moved toward her. Rosamund hurried toward him, too. He hugged her, squeezing her tight in his embrace. Then he pulled back and held her at arm's length to look her over.

"Your mother said the cruse was broken, but I didn't quite believe her."

"Believe her, Papa," she said. "It's true."

"Thank the gods you're all right!" He hugged her again. This time when he pulled back and glanced over her, it was with more of a critical eye. "What in gods' name are you wearing? And where the bloody hell did you go? We were worried about you from the moment we realized you were gone."

"I know and I am truly sorry for that. I didn't mean to worry you. Come sit down, Papa, and I will tell you."

She took him by the hand and tugged him toward the small conversation area by the hearth.

"Shall I ring for tea?" her mother asked.

"Frankly, my dear, I think I will need something stronger than tea," he muttered as he allowed Rosamund to tug him along.

They sat together. He on the long sofa piled high with cushions and pillows. She took the oversized wing-backed chair opposite him. She placed her hands in her lap, took a deep breath, and began.

"I do wish you had told me about the betrothal sooner," Rosamund said.

Guilt swept across his features for only a brief instance before he concealed it. Before he said anything, she hurried on.

"And the curse. Why didn't you tell me Queen Rowena cursed me when I was a babe?"

"We were trying to protect you," her father said. "I didn't think it was necessary to tell you because I never expected the curse to come to pass."

"Well, it did," Rosamund said. "Apparently, from what Phillip recalled, all the Fae royals bestowed a gift upon me."

Her mother came into the sitting area holding a small glass with an amber liquid. She handed it to her father. He took it from her, giving her a glance of thanks, before taking a sip.

"They all did, yes," her mother said.

Rosamund pinned her mother with her gaze. "What were they?"

"I don't think that's of any importance—" her father began.

"I'd like to know," Rosamund said.

"One queen gave you beauty, charm, and grace. One of the kings gave you strength and bravery. Another king gave you the gift of intelligence and quick wit. It was Rowena who placed the death curse upon you," her mother said. "She cursed you because—"

"I know why and that reason no longer matters. Queen Rowena thinks I'm dead. However, it was Queen Elara who reversed that curse," Rosamund said. "She came to me when I was sleeping. She told me how to break the curse."

"What do you mean came to you?" Her father scrutinized her as confusion flickered over his face.

"I don't know how she knew I was under the sleeping curse, but she appeared and told me that there was only one way to break the curse. She also told me something else, Papa. And you must listen."

Now her father's brows rose to his hairline. Rosamund scooted to the edge of her seat.

"And what is that?" he asked, genuinely interested.

"She said she knew you feared the Fae royals. But there is no need to fear them. They do not wish to conquer Stonebridge or expand their borders. She said Faery is not interested in Stonebridge lands."

He stared at her in silence for a long moment, his face devoid of emotion.

"That's very good to hear," her mother said. "Isn't it, my love?"

"How do you know she was telling you the truth?" he asked, his gaze fixed on hers.

"Why would she lie?" Rosamund said. "She had no reason to tell me a falsehood. And she told me the truth about how to break the curse."

Silence descended between them as he considered her words. He downed the amber liquid in one gulp and handed off the glass to her mother, who still stood near him.

"The curse was broken, my dear," her mother said. "Rosamund sitting here is proof of that. I believe she's right. There is no reason why Queen Elara would lie."

"Then my fears were unfounded. The spies I sent to the border lied," he said.

"Perhaps they were misled and given false information," her mother suggested. "Perhaps someone within Faery wanted a war."

"Who?" he asked.

"I should think Rowena. She is meddlesome and likes to play with people's lives, clearly," Rosamund said. "When you slighted her by not inviting her, she took out all her hate and vengeance on me."

Her father's gaze drifted back to her face. She saw the contemplation in his eyes and knew he was trying to work out how everything had happened and why.

"It appears we never needed a betrothal, either," he said. "Though why Reginald agreed to it, I have no idea. I suppose canceling the wedding was for the best."

"No," Rosamund said, the word sharp.

Her father lifted his brows in surprise. "No?"

"Tell him how the curse was broken, Rosamund," her mother said, her tone hard and firm.

He glanced from his wife to Rosamund, perplexed. "Yes. Please tell me."

Rosamund swallowed hard, her mouth suddenly dry. "Queen Elara said only one thing would break it. True love's kiss."

She said nothing else as she allowed her words to sink in. Her father leaned forward, his elbows on his knees as he peered at her with curiosity.

"True love's kiss?" he repeated.

"Yes," Rosamund said.

"And who was the one who broke it?"

"My dear, I think you know who," her mother said before she could answer.

"It was Prince Phillip," Rosamund added.

He stared at her in disbelief, then glanced up at his wife. "Prince Phillip?"

"I love him," she said. "And he loves me. And if it's all the same to you, Papa, we'd like to marry."

"Marry the prince?" he said.

"Yes, Papa."

He shot to his feet. There was color high in his cheeks. "I have already called off the wedding."

"You can speak with King Reginald," her mother said. "Tell him you made a hasty decision and that you apologize."

"I will do no such—"

"You will," her mother said, her voice stern. "And you will go this minute."

He huffed out an exasperated breath. "My darling—"

"I will have no speeches of how your diplomacy works," she interrupted, calm and cool. "You will repair relations with King Reginald. Rosamund and Phillip will marry. The wedding will go on as planned."

He stared down his wife for a long, quiet, deadly moment. Then his shoulders slumped in defeat. He looked back at Rosamund.

"You truly love him?" he asked.

She nodded. "I do."

"And he truly loves you?"

She nodded again. "He does."

He inhaled a deep breath and blew it out. "Then I suppose I have nothing left to do but speak with Reginald and make sure this wedding happens anyway."

Her mother placed the glass she still held on the table between the chairs. She grasped her father by the arm and led him toward the door. Rosamund jumped to her feet to watch as they headed for the door.

"You should. And you should go right away."

"Are you certain now is the time, my wife?"

"Yes, absolutely. Time is of the essence, my darling."

At the door, she pulled it open and ushered him out. When he was gone, she closed it behind him with a snap. She sagged against the wood door, blowing out a breath as though she had been holding it all that time. There was color high in her cheeks as her emotions ran high.

"That went well," Rosamund said.

"Yes, better than I expected. You have excellent diplomatic instincts, my daughter." She pushed off the door and walked toward her. Her gaze raked up and down her, as though seeing her for the first time. "Now, I think you should change out of those peasant clothes. Wherever did you get them?"

Rosamund smiled. She hooked her arm with her mother's. "I'll tell you the story, Mother, if you wish. But first, I'd love a hot bath and a meal. I'm ravenous!"

"Ah, yes, of course. I'll ring for the servants." She released her daughter and headed for the gold cord, then halted and turned back. A smile exploded on her face. "My daughter is getting married."

A flush of joy, hot and wild, went over Rosamund.

"And," her mother added, "I could not be more pleased. I'm so happy for you, Rosamund."

Rosamund was happy, too. She could not wait to share the news with Phillip.

Queen Rowena sat high in her castle as satisfaction oozed from her pores. She had finally gotten her revenge on the hateful King Stephan. His daughter was dead by her hand. It had been a very long eighteen years, but she was happy to finally have her vengeance.

As she lounged on her throne drinking a glass of her favorite elderberry wine, Ferrin arrived. She had sent him on an errand for her to make sure the prince took the dead princess back to her father. She wanted to know the king's reaction when he realized his only daughter was dead. She sat straight up and poured another glass of celebratory wine.

"Ah, Ferrin. You have returned. What news from Myst Hall do you have for me?"

His face was pale. He stood before her with his hand clenched and a look that told her she was not going to like what he had to say. Immediately, her mood darkened.

"Well?" she asked.

"Your majesty, the prince returned to Myst Hall with the princess," he began.

But she sensed something was wrong. Her hand tightened into a fist, her nails biting into her palm. "And?"

"And it seems the princess did not die when she pricked her finger." The boy swallowed hard, his throat working.

Rowena lifted her head and looked down her nose at him. "What do you mean she didn't die?"

"It appears, my queen, she was under a sleeping curse."

Fury erupted behind her eyes. She flung the goblet she'd been holding across the room. Wine splashed out as it clattered to the ground with a resounding clang. She rose to her full height, taking a deep breath to steady her rage.

"Someone altered my spell. Someone from one of the other Courts," she said, her voice low and dangerous. "I will not rest until I discover who that was. My vengeance will be swift and deadly."

"Yes, my queen." Ferrin bowed his head low. "There is more news, my queen."

She turned her dark gaze on him. "More?"

"The curse was broken." His voice was a low whisper as though he were terrified to tell her.

She clenched both fists tight. "Broken you say."

"Yes, my queen."

Her breath quickened as she stood there, staring at the young Fae who had brought her this dark and terrible news.

"Be gone," she said with a wave of her hand.

It was best she dismissed him before she released her fury on him. He scurried out of the room. As he did so, she knew what she had to do.

She had to pay King Stephan a visit once more.

Chapter 30

The days passed in a whirlwind. After her father reconciled with King Reginald, wedding preparations began at an accelerated pace. Royal decrees went out announcing the upcoming nuptials to both Woodhaven and Myst inviting the nobility and the gentry. There was some debate on whether to invite the Fae royals, but Rosamund had decided she'd had enough faery magic in her life and so the matter was dropped.

Much to her dismay, she hadn't seen much of Phillip in the preparation days. Only a few moments in passing. She missed him. She wanted to tell him everything and nothing and she wondered what he was doing while she was off having wedding gown fittings and brunches and meetings with the royal baker about the wedding cake.

Her mother kept her busy with other engagements with the ladies of the nobility including Queen Adele. Rosamund suspected it was her clever way of keeping her away from Phillip before the wedding.

Rosamund wasn't interested in the wedding cake or what food would be served at the reception afterward. She was only interested in marrying Phillip.

Apparently, there was also a lively debate about where the new-lyweds would live. Her father wanted to build a small cottage for them near Myst Hall. King Reginald wanted to commission a castle for them near Haven Castle. Neither agreed on the final destination.

When Rosamund heard of the great debate, she asked, "Why not both? We can split our time between kingdoms."

The solution was agreed upon by both kings. Immediately, plans were drawn up for each home to begin the building process.

Initially, the wedding was to take place inside the royal chapel, but the list of attendees grew exponentially daily. There was simply not enough room inside the small Myst Hall chapel for the entire congregation who wanted to witness the marriage. So, it was de-cided they would move the ceremony outside to the royal gardens where there was an abundance of spring flowers in bloom allowing for the perfect backdrop.

An arbor was erected at the far end of the garden. The lattice was covered with greenery and flowers climbing up and over the top. Gossamer curtains were attached to each side, giving it a romantic look and feel. Her mother had the last say in the décor including flowers and approved the arbor with a wistful smile.

Everything was coming together. It was all perfection.

Guests began to arrive. Too many to house them all in the castle save for a few of the highest nobles which included King Reginald's brother who was a duke. Rosamund caught bits and pieces of conversation about where to house them all and how many more chairs they would need for the outdoor affair. There was even talk about who would attend the post-wedding reception and limiting the guest list to only the highest ranking in both kingdoms.

Rosamund was not interested in any of that detail. She left it in her mother's capable hands.

The night before the wedding, she was banished to her bedchamber, forbidden to see Phillip. Her mother felt it was bad luck for her to see him before the wedding. She spent her time roaming the area of her rooms, trying to find something to occupy her mind. She was too restless to sleep. Butterflies were in her stomach with the excitement of the coming day.

She paused a moment to stare at the gown on the dress form, her heart ramming hard in her throat. It was the most beautiful gown she had ever seen. It was a deep shade of green damask silk and the softest material she had ever touched with bell sleeves and a three-foot train. She had never seen so much beautiful material on one dress in her life. Across the neckline of the bodice was intricate beadwork that sparkled and must have taken hours for someone to sew in place.

Her mother's eyes pooled with tears when she put it on for her final fitting. She said the gown brought out the color of her eyes.

She ran a hand down the length of the gown and sighed with appreciation. As she stood there staring at it, imagining wearing it, there was a knock on her door. Startled, she stared at it in shock for a long moment. The knock sounded again. She hurried to it, wondering who would be visiting her so late in the evening. Who would the guards allow to visit her?

When she cracked open the door, a man in a hooded cloak stood on the other side in the hallway. His hands were clasped behind his back as though he held something.

"Yes?" Suspicion lanced through her.

He pushed the hood up a bit to keep the guards on either side from seeing his face. But she saw who it was. A grin erupted.

"Can I help you?" she added, trying to sound official and not alert the guards.

Jeffrey brought his hand from behind his back. He held one single white rose. She gasped.

"For you, your highness, and a message," he said. "A rose for a Rose. I was asked to make sure you received it."

Her heart thundered as she took it, wondering where he had managed to find a single white rose. There were no rosebushes in the castle gardens nor anywhere near the castle. She made a note to ask him when they were alone.

"Do you know the significance of a white rose, your highness?" he asked. When she shook her head, he continued. "It means everlasting love and devotion."

Hearing that made her knees go weak. She gripped the door jamb with her free hand as the blood whooshed out of her head. She glanced down at the single rose, the perfect petals, and her heart swelled.

"I will wear it tomorrow," she said. She vowed to find a glass of water or something to put it in so it wouldn't wilt before the morning.

"His highness the prince hoped you would." He granted her a smile and a quick bow of his head. "Any return message for his highness?"

She thought about that for a moment until finally she nodded. "Yes. Tell him I look forward to our next adventure together."

"As the lady commands." He bowed once again and then hurried away.

Rosamund closed the door and leaned against it, smelling the sweet scent of the rose. As she held it, she noticed one thing in particular.

There were no thorns.

She laid awake for several hours until at some point, she drifted off into exhaustion. It seemed she had just closed her eyes when there was a commotion in her bedchamber and someone was shaking her awake.

When she opened her eyes, the first thing she saw was the white rose in the glass of water by her bedside. She smiled as soon as she saw it.

One of the maids bustled in to rouse her and help her dress for the day. She made a note to come back and retrieve the rose before she left her bedchamber.

The gown was perfection. She stood before the long mirror and gaped, hardly recognizing herself. Her mother bustled in, her reflection behind Rosamund in the mirror. Her mother wore a gown in a deep blue with a full skirt and sleeves that came to a point on her hands. Her hair was pulled up in an elaborate style on her head with a small spray of flowers over one ear. Rosamund couldn't help but think how radiant her mother looked.

The queen pressed her fingertips to her lips, a dreamy look of admiration on her face.

"I knew that color would be stunning on you," she said.

"I don't think stunning is the right word," Queen Adele said, pausing behind her mother in a swish of skirts.

Queen Adele was dressed in a gown of violet. Like her mother, her hair was coiled around her head, curls piled high, and a sprig of flowers behind her ear. She gave her an appreciative smile as she looked at Rosamund.

"The gown is beautiful, Mother." She turned to face her. "I love it."

Queen Adele handed her the bouquet with a mixture of flowers. "We're here to escort you to your father."

Rosamund remembered the white flower beside her bed. "One moment, please."

She hurried back into her chamber. Relief washed over her when she saw it still in the glass. She took it, placing it in the center of her bouquet to make sure Phillip would see it. Smiling, she returned to the waiting queens. Together, the three of them left behind her bedchamber and headed for the castle gardens.

Her father, as well as King Reginald, flanked the exit to the gardens. They were both dressed in their finest attire. Her father in indigo to match her mother. Reginald in violet to match his wife. A smile crossed her father's face as she paused next to him.

"You look lovely," he said.

Reginald said, "More than lovely. She's a stunning beauty! My son is a lucky man." He reached for her, kissed her on each cheek. His face was lit with delighted joy.

"Thank you," Rosamund said.

Her father held his arm out to her. She wrapped her hand in the crook of his elbow trying to ignore the nerves erupting through her stomach. Queen Adele took her husband's arm. Together, they started down the long aisle to the altar where the High Bishop and Phillip waited. Her mother gave them once last glance as she followed the other two. She and her father stepped up to the doorway. Rosamund got a first glance of the assemblage and stifled a gasp.

There were so many people filled in every chair from the front to the back. All rose to their feet and turned toward the door, waiting for her. Near the front of the altar, she was certain she spied the four Fae Royals. Two kings, two queens.

"Are you ready?" he asked, a smile in his voice.

"There are so many people," she whispered. "The Fae royals came? I thought they weren't invited."

"I had a change of heart. Honestly, I was surprised they came."

Her gut suddenly clenched. "What about Queen Rowena?"

"She was invited but declined," he said.

Something about that seemed off to her, but she refrained from saying so. If Rowena didn't know she was alive and well, she certainly did now. What would stop her from coming after her again? She tried to put that out of her mind as she stared at the large congregation. Her stomach clenched into a tighter knot.

"I knew there were going to be a lot but I didn't expect...this."

He patted her hand. "You only need to concern yourself with one person." When she cut him a glance, he smiled and said, "Phillip."

Yes, Phillip. She turned her gaze back to the aisle and saw him waiting for her at the end of the altar. He wore dark pants and shiny knee-high black boots. His violet waistcoat was the same color as his parent's wedding clothing. His sword was strapped to his side. From the distance, she could see the gold buttons gleaming in the late morning sun. He even wore white gloves to complete the formal attire. Her heart skipped a beat.

She took a deep breath, expelled it. "I'm ready."

They started down the aisle together. It was only as she took her first step, she realized there was lute and harp music. Had there been music decided in the planning? She didn't recall. All eyes were on her as she and her father made their way toward the altar awash in morning sun.

But as they continued, a shadow passed over the gardens, momentarily blotting out the light. Her breath caught in her throat as she stole a glance upward. But there was nothing in the sky.

Then she heard it. The *whump, whump* of wings as the shadow once again passed over them. She glanced upward and saw the black leathery beast gliding through the sky, circling the gardens as though it were a predator stalking its prey.

She came to a jarring halt halfway down the aisle, her gaze fixed on the sky as she watched the great black dragon. When others caught sight of it, a ripple of gasps went through the crowd.

"What is it?" her father asked.

"Dragon," she whispered.

"Nonsense. There are no dragons here," he said.

"But there are."

She never looked away as the dragon—Rowena—landed on the outer wall with a resounding boom. Rocks crumbled to the ground in her wake.

"What a lovely gathering you have, King Stephan," the great beast said in a deep, raspy voice. "Such a glittering affair."

Her serpentine eyes landed on Stephan as she lowered her head to look closer to the king. Rosamund moved to stand in front of her father, clutching her bouquet tight in one hand and wishing she had a weapon in the other. Phillip moved to stand by her side, pushing the king behind him. The two of them formed a human wall between the king and the dragon.

Most of the crowd had scattered back into the castle, leaving only a few remaining. The four Fae royals stood front and center. Both Fae kings, Atlas and Draco, wielded their swords. Elara and Titania flanked them. Titania's hands glowed with a bright white light. King Reginald took his wife by the hand and rushed away from the front of the altar as quickly as possible. Adele cut them a glance, fear etched on her face.

"I see my fellow Fae have also joined the celebration. A pity I will have to roast them alive as well."

The dragon's throat burned white hot as she opened her snout and prepared to release a stream of fire. Titania jumped in front of them, holding her hands aloft and forming a glittering shield around them all.

This did nothing but infuriate the dragon more. She growled, low in her throat, making the wall in which she sat rumble. More loose rocks fell to the ground.

"Be gone, Rowena!" Titania said. "You are not wanted here."

The dragon beast lifted straight and tall, her short stubby front leg clutching her heart as though she were offended.

"Not wanted?" Then she laughed and steam trickled from her snout. "My dear queen, I was invited as an honored guest."

"Not you." Stephan pushed around Rosamund and Phillip and stood his ground between them and the dragon. "The Queen of the Eternal Court, Rowena, was invited."

Her eyes narrowed to slits. "I *am* the Queen of the Eternal Court."

She made to breathe another jet of fire toward her father. Rosamund cried out just as Phillip shoved the king out of the way, then spun and tackled her to the ground. The bouquet flew out of her hand as the blaze went over their heads, setting a few chairs on fire.

Titania was at their side in an instant, helping Rosmund to her feet. Phillip helped the king up. The other three Fae stood their ground, facing the dragon.

"What do you want?" Stephan asked.

"Want? Why...I want the princess *dead*. She should be dead!"

"I changed the curse," Elara said, stepping forward.

Seeing that act of bravery made Rosamund's gut clench into a tight knot. She wanted to cry out to her, tell her to step away from the beast, but Titania shook her head, urging her to keep quiet.

"Oh, of course, the Celestial Queen would be the one to foil all my plans. *You will pay.*" She readied another burst of dragon fire.

Elara, though, stood her ground, raising her hands to the sky and chanting something in the Fae language under her breath. Rosamund couldn't hear what it was. Suddenly, the sun was blotted out by a swath of clouds. What appeared to be stardust rained down from the sky in slashes of bright white and yellow light. It pounded Rowena's dragon form. Each time a beam hit her scaly skin, it left a sizzle behind.

She cried out in pain and then took to the skies, flying up and away. Elara dropped her hands and turned to the couple, the king, and Titania. She rushed over and gripped Rosamund by the upper arms.

"You must leave this place at once," she urged.

"And go where?" Rosamund asked. "There is no place she will not find me."

"The girl is quite right," Titania said, turning to her fellow queen. "We must find a way to stop her."

Overhead, Rowena circled, made another pass, and headed for the castle once more.

"What can we do?" Phillip asked.

The dragon landed again, this time crushing the altar and destroying the once-beautiful arbor with a swish of her tail. Flowers flew in all directions.

"We must fight back."

Even as Titania said it, Atlas and Draco went into action. But there was no stopping the dragon. One swipe of her massive tail and King Atlas went flying across the garden. He landed on the ground, skidding to a halt at the base of a tree. Draco tried to fight her next, but he met a similar fate.

Phillip unsheathed his sword. He turned to her. "Rose, get back inside the castle. Get to safety."

"I can't leave you—"

"GO."

Titania grabbed her by the hand and led her back up the aisle the way she'd come. She glanced back over her shoulder to see Phillip and her father, who had also wielded his sword, charge toward Rowena. When the great dragon readied another fire burst, she skidded to a halt, trying desperately to pull her hand free from the Fae queen's grasp. She held tight.

"No, princess!" the queen warned.

"My father!"

A burst of fire from the dragon. King Stephan saw it in time, though, and dove out of the way, dropped to the ground and rolled. But the action cost him. He lost his sword. It was on the ground too far for him to reach.

Phillip shouted something and suddenly Jeffrey and Charles were at his side, also armed with swords. Rosamund wasn't sure where the brothers were sitting, but it was clear they were not going to let the prince fight the dragon alone.

Jeffrey and Charles ran between the back legs of the dragon, swinging their swords and slicing the back of her legs as they went.

She lifted her head to the heavens and bellowed a loud roar. The great beast stumbled backward, crashing into the wall. It crumbled under her weight.

Rowena rolled to one side, her huge body crushing flowers and felling trees. She came back up on her back legs but that gave Phillip enough time to charge.

The Fae queen took Rosamund by the hand again and tugged her away from the fight. But as she did so, her father stumbled into sight. There was a large gash on the side of his head. Blood streamed down his face as he hobbled toward them.

"Papa!"

Rosamund jerked free of the queen and ran toward her father. He stumbled as he reached her. She caught him in her arms keeping him on his feet. He leaned into her, accepting her help.

"I'll be fine," he said when he saw her concerned expression.

"We have to get you to a healer," she said, clutching him tight.

"I need to help Phillip." He tried to return to the fight, but Rosamund held fast.

"No—"

"Listen, both of you," the queen interrupted. "There is a weakness under her wing, near the joint."

"A weakness?" Stephan asked, his brows pinched together.

"You mean like a soft spot? The only place her scales aren't," Rosamund said.

She nodded. "Stabbing her there should subdue her."

"But it won't kill her," Rosamund said.

"I don't think so. Once she is subdued, we will be able to capture her and return her to Faery," Titania said.

"Phillip needs to know," the princess said. She watched as he, Jeffrey, Charles and the two Fae kings fought the dragon. Rowena destroyed everything in her path.

"What's stopping her from burning down the castle?" Stephan asked.

Titania's cobalt gaze stared down at the dragon who stumbled back and forth, as though she were drunk.

"Her power is fading. She must not have enough fire power to do more damage."

"Then I need to get a message to Phillip," her father said.

He started to go, but Rosamund caught him by the arm. "No. You're injured." She paused, gazing down at the melee. "I'll go."

"Rosamund, I will not allow it—"

"She won't expect me to be there," she interrupted. She turned to the Fae queen. "Please protect my father."

Her gaze flickered from her to Stephan and back again. Finally, she gave a nod. "As you wish, princess. But be warned. Her breath is like poison and can render you immobile."

Nodding and without waiting for any more objections, Rosamund ran up the aisle.

CHAPTER 31

Rosamund cursed her long gown as she hurried trying hard not to step on it. She spied her father's sword on the ground and swept it up, clutching it tight in her sweaty palm. She charged forward.

The dragon used her massive claw to swipe first Jeffrey then Charles out of the way. They both went flying in different directions, landing on the ground with a groan. Both Fae kings were rendered unconscious by the beast. Rosamund sucked in a sharp breath as she watched Rowena go after Phillip next. Her razor-sharp claws cut through the air, missing him as he ducked.

"Phillip!"

He cut her a glance, his expression morphing from surprise to worry. "Get back to the castle."

Rowena caught sight of her and reared back, her head held high as she looked down her massive snout at the two of them. Rosamund halted next to Phillip who immediately wrapped his arm around her. He held his sword in his other hand, as if ready to strike.

"Ah, the perfect couple. Isn't this wonderful?" She lowered her head, her dragon eyes peering at them both. "I should have killed you both when I had the chance."

The beast inhaled a breath. Rosamund knew immediately what she planned to do.

"Her breath—!" she started.

Phillip shoved her out of the way as the dragon puffed out a white cloud. Rosamund stumbled and fell, her gown ripping and the sword falling from her hand. When she looked back over her shoulder, the cloud had consumed Phillip. She let out a strangled cry as he stumbled from the right to the left and then tumbled to the ground. His sword fell out of his hand.

The dragon laughed her smokey laugh. Then she turned her gaze on Rosamund.

"It's the two of us now, princess. Don't think I'll be letting you get away."

Rosamund climbed to her feet. Her gown was covered in dirt and grass stains. The hem was ripped. She lifted her gaze to the great dragon, her hands clutched at her side.

I am not afraid.

She spied her father's sword gleaming in the morning sun. Just beyond that was Phillip's. Two swords.

Rowena sucked in another breath. Rosamund took that moment to bolt into a run. She grabbed her father's sword off the ground in one fluid motion, then made for Phillip's. She snatched it up in her other hand. She spun to face the dragon as the beast puffed out another breath.

Rosamund ran as fast as she could but she tripped on her skirt and fell forward. She released the weapons as she landed on the ground so hard it jarred her to the back of her teeth. The puff of smoke went over her, missing her.

Without waiting for the dragon to regroup, she rolled to a sitting position and ripped away the remaining skirt to give her feet freedom of movement. Then she scrambled to her feet and snatched up both of the swords once more. Behind her, she thought she heard her mother cry out and her father shout her name. She ignored them both and ran directly toward the dragon.

Rowena saw her coming and stumbled backward to get her in her line of sight. Rosamund glanced up a moment to see a faint glow in her chest, as though her magic returned and she was able to breath fire once again.

The princess eyed the dragon's wings, looking for the weak spot Titania mentioned. She spotted the leathery looking skin just under the joint where there were no scales to protect her. That was where she needed to stab her.

Taking a deep breath, she ran again right for the dragon. Rowena stumbled backward, trying to get her in her sights, but Rosamund was fast. Unhindered by her skirt, she was able to run at a quicker speed. Holding both swords, though, slowed her down. She dropped her father's and held onto to Phillip's with both hands.

The dragon realized what she was doing and took a swipe with her large claw. The tips grazed Rosamund's back as she tumbled to the ground, a shout of pain escaping her. She rolled to her back as the dragon planted both feet on either side of her. Her massive snout was inches from her face. Hot steam came out in puffs from her large nostrils.

"You think you can defeat me, don't you, girl?"

When the dragon spoke, Rosamund was very aware of her spiky teeth. One chomp and she was dead. She felt the ground for the sword but came up empty handed.

"Why do you want me dead?" Rosamund asked.

The dragon blinked, as though the question surprised her.

"Killing me solves nothing," she hurried on. "Just because you were slighted doesn't mean I should die."

The dragon huffed out a hot breath. Rosamund closed her eyes and turned her head as the steamy air cascaded over her.

"You're right," the dragon said then. "The king must die instead."

With that, she shoved her huge body upward, moving away from Rosamund and peering through the destroyed gardens for her father.

Rosamund realized, too late, her mistake.

Rowena the dragon lumbered toward the castle, her chest glowing as she built up enough fire to release a fiery stream.

She climbed to her feet, scanning the area for the swords. But suddenly one of the Fae kings was at her side holding one arm that appeared to be limp against his chest. In his other hand, he held a dagger out to her.

"Here. Try this. And hurry."

She snatched the dagger out of his hand without a thanks and darted up the aisle toward the dragon. The dagger was much lighter in her hand than either sword and she felt as though she had a shot.

The only thing that helped her catch up to the dragon was that she was big, slow, and blood streamed down the backs of her legs where Jeffrey and Charles had cut her. Her tail swished back and forth. Rosamund zig-zagged to avoid it. When she finally caught up to her, she ran ahead, her legs throbbing and burning with the exertion. She skittered to a halt in front of Rowena when she was only a few feet from the castle.

"Rowena!"

The beast halted, her head swiveling down to look at her.

"You are a determined thing, aren't you?"

Her chest still glowed faintly, as though she were still building up the fire down within her core. Then she leaned closer to Rosamund, her snout only inches away from her face. It was the opportunity she needed.

She darted forward, her heart in her throat, as she clutched the dagger. Before Rowena realized what was happening, Rosamund shoved the dagger hard inside the soft place under her wing.

The dragon emitted a shrill growl as she reared upward. Rosamund staggered away from her, watching in horror as the dragon stumbled and fell to the ground with a thunderous noise, making it shake.

"You vile little creature!" she cried out.

She flopped from side to side, as if trying to reach the dagger sticking out of her side but couldn't. Titania used that moment to step forward, her hands outstretched and glowing. Elara joined her. The two of them used their Fae magic to surround Rowena with their white glowing magic and force her to transform back into her Fae form. The dagger was sticking out from under her arm.

Titania moved closer and kneeled down to look at the dark Fae queen.

"Your rule is over, Rowena. You will face your fate at the Tribunal. When you are found guilty, you will spend the rest of your immortal days imprisoned in the Eternal Tower."

Dark menace crossed the other queen's face as she glared up at Titania. Then she said something in her Fae language and spat.

The two Fae kings joined them. Draco held a length of rope in his hands. With Rowena subdued by Titania's and Elara's magic, he wound the rope around her wrists and tied it with a tight knot. King Atlas took her by the upper arm and hoisted her to her feet.

"Atlas and I will make sure she's properly guarded," Draco said.

The two Fae queens released their magic hold.

"See that you do," Titania said, her voice stern.

And then the three of them disappeared out of sight.

As soon as they were gone, Rosamund broke into a run toward Phillip. She dropped to her knees by his side and scooped him into her arms, cradling his head against her chest. She brushed away a lock of hair on his forehead. His eyes were still closed as he groaned, his brows drawing together as if he were in pain.

"I'm here," she whispered. "Your Rose."

Finally, he opened his honey-colored eyes, his gaze meeting hers. Her heart tripped in her chest as relief sputtered through her. She smiled.

"Rose...what happened? The last thing I remember was a cloud of smoke."

"She blew her breath on you and it knocked you out," she said. "But you're all right now. The threat is over. The dragon is gone."

"Gone?" He pushed out of her arms to a sitting position and then immediately grunted. He put his head in his hands. "Where is she?"

"Take care, prince. The effects of her dragon's breath will take a bit to wear off," Queen Titania said as she gazed down at the two of them.

Phillip shook his head to clear it, then looked up at the queen. Question creased his face.

"Where is Rowena?" he asked.

"Vanquished. She will face trial for her misdeeds at the Tribunal. And then she will be punished," the Fae queen said.

Rosamund helped him to his feet, then. He glanced around at the destruction. The royal gardens had been decimated by Rowena's dragon fire. Their wedding arbor was shattered in pieces. The chairs were scattered everywhere. Trees were down. Plants were flattened. The ground was scorched in places.

"Oh..." he said on a breath as he took in the sight.

"I'll all right," Rose said quickly. Her voice wobbled only a little.

"All right? Rose, the wedding—"

"We will find another place to marry," she said, trying to sound hopeful. Though, in truth, seeing the devastation around her was disheartening.

Then he took in her appearance, glancing down at her ripped and soiled gown. His face contorted in pain. "Your gown..."

"It's fine." She waved away her concern. Because if she didn't, she would break into tears over the ruination of her beautiful gown.

"No, it's not," he said, stepping away from her. "There has to be some way to repair it."

"Well, there is a way," Titania said. "If you'll allow it."

Rosamund cut her a glance as Elara joined her. She nodded. "Yes, please."

A smile creased her beautiful face. She cast a questioning glance at the other Fae queen who gave her a nod. They clasped hands and closed their eyes. Together, a power formed between them. A bright, blue-white glow began to surge from them and then covered Rosamund. Her skin tickled as the sparkling radiance overcame her. She watched, fascinated, as the threads of her gown reformed and repaired. After a moment, the light faded and she was standing there once again in her beautiful green wedding gown.

She was unable to hide her gasp of delight. "You did it."

"Of course, we did," Elara said. "You are truly a fairy princess now, dearest."

"Rose, your skin is...sparkling," Phillip said, wonder in his voice.

She glanced down to see her skin was, indeed, shimmering in the late morning sun.

"Our work here is finished," Titania said.

"Finished?" Phillip asked.

"When we were invited to the wedding, we suspected Rowena would also arrive and exact her revenge," Elara said. "Since she would know the princess was not dead as she had expected."

"We hoped, of course, that was not the case," Titania said. "It was why the four of us decided to come. I'm only sorry we did not act sooner."

"We will do everything in our power to make sure Rowena never again releases her dark magic on anyone," Elara added.

"And we appreciate that, your majesties," Phillip said with a low bow. "Thank you for your help."

"We should have helped more," Titania said. "Now, we must take our leave and see to the Tribunal."

They both bowed to Phillip and Rosamund. They returned the bow.

"Farewell," Rosamund said.

And then they disappeared in a puff of faery magic.

Jeffrey and Charles joined them, then, looking as though they'd both been run over by an oxen cart.

"Oh," Rosamund exclaimed.

"By the gods, man, you both look awful," Phillip said.

"We both feel awful," Jeffrey said. A grim expression crossed his face.

"I thought that dragon was going to be the death of me," Charles said.

"The death of all of us," Phillip added.

Her parents along with King Reginald and Queen Adele arrived then, relieved to see all of them still alive and in one piece.

"I suppose we will need to reschedule the wedding," Phillip said.

"We can still have a wedding," her father said.

"We can?" Rosamund's head snapped in his direction.

"Of course, we can," he said. "We have a chapel, don't we?"

"But, my darling, what about all the guests?" her mother asked.

"We will just have to make do," Stephan said. He gave his wife a large, joyful grin, as if this was the best idea he'd ever had. "Bring those of the highest rank into the chapel, find the bishop, and let's get these two married."

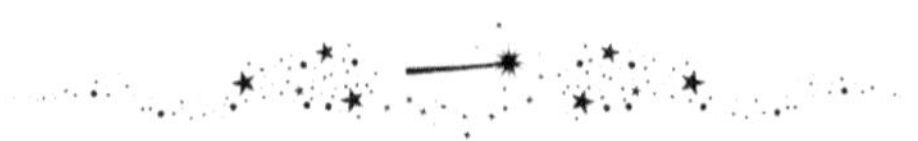

Rosamund was grateful to the Fae queen for repairing her gown. It had pained her to rip the skirt when she was fighting against Rowena.

Her father's head injury was tended by the healer, who managed to stop the bleeding and bandage him.

After some confusion and a bit of chaos, that evening, the chapel was filled with those who arrived to witness the wedding of Rosamund and Phillip. She still hadn't a moment to thank him for the white rose which, miraculously, survived along with the other flowers in her bouquet.

Once more, she stood at the end of the aisle, holding her father's arm, and facing the altar that had quickly been decorated with candelabras to give it a romantic glow. Her mother and Queen Adele did what they could on short notice.

At the end of the aisle, Phillip waited in his finery that was still smudged with dirt. He seemed unconcerned with his attire and only had eyes for her as they started their journey down the aisle. Her heart beat in anticipation, her nerves suddenly gone. She was focused solely on Phillip's smile and the way the candlelight reflected in the strands of his hair turning them gold.

At the altar, her father kissed her cheek, the sheer joy evident in his face. She took Phillip's outstretched hand. Together they turned to the bishop and pledged their love and life to each other forevermore.

Afterward, at the celebration of their nuptials, Phillip grasped her hand and stole her away from the grand dining hall onto the balcony to get a breath of evening air. Stars twinkled overhead in an indigo sky. The full moon shone brightly, the beams cascading down in slashes of blue-white light.

"Are you happy?" he asked.

"Yes. Are you?"

He turned to her, taking both her hands in his. "Deliriously so. I'm glad you got the white rose."

"You noticed." She grinned up at him. "I didn't have a chance to tell you. Jeffrey told me the meaning. Everlasting love and de-votion."

Thinking of it now made her heart squeeze.

"I hoped he would. I mean it, too." He squeezed her hands. "Rose...I'm so grateful for everything we went through to find each other."

She loved that his nickname for her was Rose. Once it had irritated her. Now, she wouldn't want him to call her anything else.

She leaned into him to steal some of his warmth as a cool wind breezed over her.

"As am I. Even falling under the sleeping curse."

"*Especially* falling under the sleeping curse. If you hadn't, things may have turned out much differently for us. Oh, and I wanted to give you this."

He reached into his pocket.

"Hold out your hand."

She gave him a quizzical look but obliged. He dropped the gold coin into her palm. She emitted a small gasp as she eyed it, the shiny gold surface winking in the evening light.

"The gold coin. You still had it."

"I kept it for you."

He wrapped his arms around her, pulling her close into his embrace. She tipped her head upward to look into those breathtaking honey-colored eyes of his.

"What shall we do now, my prince?"

"Perhaps we find a new adventure, princess." A smile pulled at the corner of his mouth.

"Where shall we go to find this new adventure?" She slid her arms around his waist, loving the way his strong body felt against hers.

His smile widened. "Wherever the wind takes us."

When he kissed her, his lips warm and gentle on hers, she couldn't wait to find out where the wind took them.

Epilogue

"And they lived happily ever after," Hilde said.

Marigold sighed with a blissful contentment about the story of a sleeping beauty, a handsome prince, and a dark faery with the ability to transform into a dragon. It had given her such joy to tell the story of Rosamund and Phillip. She was very fond of them, after all.

"Did they have more adventures?" Marigold asked.

"They certainly did. Many more. And they loved each other very much."

Another wistful sigh. "Someday my prince will come."

She paused a moment before she replied. There were so many things she wanted to tell her niece, but couldn't. Not yet. "Of course, he will."

"How will I know when he does?" With her chin still on her knees, she tilted her head to look at her.

"Oh, you'll know," she replied with a knowing smile. "You'll feel it."

"Where?" Marigold asked.

Hilde tapped her chest over her heart. "Here. And sometimes in your gut."

"You mean like a gut feeling?"

The girl was always so full of questions after she finished a tale. Hilde nodded. "Exactly."

She said nothing for a long moment, her mind working as she thought about the story and everything that happened. Finally, she asked, "Whatever happened to the dark faery?"

"She was sentenced to life imprisonment in the Eternal Tower at the Tribunal," Hilde said.

"Forever?"

She nodded. "Forever."

That was not the end of Rowena's story. It was widely known the Fae were immortal, powerful creatures of both the light and the dark. Rowena's immortal life would not be lived out in the darkest depths of the Eternal Tower within the far reaches of the realm of Faery.

But that was a story for another day.

She glanced at her watch and was surprised at the time. It was late evening now and had been hours since Linnea bought up a tray of food for them.

"Now, Miss Marigold, it's time to sleep for tomorrow we have a busy day."

The girl's face darkened as a frown appeared. It was clear to her the girl was not looking forward to the funeral. Hilde understood. It was hard on both her and Linnea.

"I know. I promised." Her gaze lifted and she reached out a hand. Hilde grasped it, holding it tight. "You will still be there?"

"As I promised," she said with a reassuring smile.

She refused to release her hand. "Auntie, what will happen at the funeral?"

"The funeral is a time for those who loved your father to honor and celebrate him. To remember him as he was when he was alive. Not how he died. It's a time to comfort each other while we grieve for him. And it's a chance to say a final farewell."

That seemed to comfort her. A sense of peace crossed her face as she released her hand. She stretched out her legs and scooted down into the bed. Hilde reached over and brushed a lock of her sunny blonde hair off her face.

"Good night, sweet girl."

"Good night," she said around a yawn.

Hilde made her way out of the girl's room, closing the door softly behind her. She paused there a long moment, leaning against the door. Whenever she told these stories to her, it was almost as though she relived them. Almost as though she were back there once again in that enchanted realm. How she missed it.

Someday, she would tell Marigold the truth of her heritage. It would have to be the right time. Now was not that time. When she was ready. When she told her enough stories and the girl believed.

For, after all, fairy tales really did come true.

ALSO BY MICHELLE MILES

Age of Wizards (Epic Fantasy)

In the Tower of the Wizard King

On the Hunt for the Wizard King

Dragon Protectors (Paranormal Shifter Romance)

Desiring the Dragon Lord

Seducing the Dragon Knight

Tempting Her Dragon Bodyguard

Dragon Protectors Book Collection, Books 1-3

Dream Walker (Urban Fantasy)

Call of the Dark

Blood and Bone

Flame and Fury

Smoke and Ashes

Light of the World

Dream Walker Collection (Books 1-5)

Dream Walker: Origins (Fantasy)

Provenance

Enchanted Realms (Fantasy Romance)

Once Upon a Midnight Clear

Once Upon True Love's Kiss

Once Upon an Enchanted Kiss

Five Towers (YA Fantasy)

The Sorcerer's Daughter

**Ransom & Fortune Adventures
(Time Travel Action/Adventure)**

Highland Fling, Vol 1

Dead of Winter, Vol 2

The Citadel, Vol 3

Lord of the Underworld, Vol 4

Realm of Honor (Fantasy Romance)

One Knight Only

Only for a Knight

A Knight to Remember

A Knight Like No Other

Shadows of the Knight

Realm of Honor Collection (Books 1-5)

Guardians of Atlantis (Fantasy Romance)

Tempting Eden

Seducing Eve

Ravishing Helene

Guardians of Atlantis Box Set

Shorts and Anthologies (Fantasy/Paranormal)

A Dance Among the Faeries, Short Story

Eorwulf, Short Story

The Soul of Sharah, Short Story

Sinfully Sweet, Short Story

Flights of Fantasy: A Collection of Short Stories

About the Author

MICHELLE MILES believes in fairy tales, true love and magic. She writes heart-stopping urban fantasy, epic fantasy and paranormal romance with an action/adventure twist that will leave you breathless. She is the author of numerous series that includes everything from angels and demons to fairies, dragons and elves.

She is a member of Romance Writers of America (RWA) and Science Fiction and Fantasy Writers Association (SFWA). A native Texan, in her spare time she loves reading, listening to music, watching movies, hiking, and drinking wine. She can be found online at Facebook, Instagram, Pinterest and Goodreads.

Your Adventure Awaits

Read more at MichelleMiles.net